"Ever think it would get this steamy between us?" he asked.

"It's all the hot air you're spewing," she said, but remembered how many times she had imagined them in steamier situations. The thought caused a tightening deep within her body. "I thought you were the man who didn't want to get involved with anyone?"

"What you want and what happens aren't always the same."

"And now you're going to tell me I'm irresistible?" She did look at him then, certain he was teasing her. The seriousness of his expression bothered her. Quickly, she looked forward again.

"I don't know what's going on," he said.

Neither did she.

"I'd like to explore it," he added.

WHAT ARE *LOVESWEPT* ROMANCES?

They are stories of true romance and touching emotion. We believe those two very important ingredients are constants in our highly sensual and very believable stories in the LOVE-SWEPT line. Our goal is to give you, the reader, stories of consistently high quality that may sometimes make you laugh, sometimes make you cry, but are always fresh and creative and contain many delightful surprises within their pages.

Most romance fans read an enormous number of books. Those they truly love, they keep. Others may be traded with friends and soon forgotten. We hope that each LOVESWEPT romance will be a treasure—a "keeper." We will always try to publish

LOVE STORIES YOU'LL NEVER FORGET
BY AUTHORS YOU'LL ALWAYS REMEMBER

The Editors

DESTINY
STRIKES
TWICE

MARIS
SOULE

BANTAM BOOKS
NEW YORK · TORONTO · LONDON · SYDNEY · AUCKLAND

DESTINY STRIKES TWICE

A Bantam Book / September 1996

ISBN 0-553-44529-4

Published simultaneously in the United States and Canada

Bantam Books are published by Bantam Books, a division of Bantam Doubleday Dell Publishing Group, Inc. Its trademark, consisting of the words "Bantam Books" and the portrayal of a rooster, is Registered in U.S. Patent and Trademark Office and in other countries. Marca Registrada. Bantam Books, 1540 Broadway, New York, New York 10036.

PRINTED IN THE UNITED STATES OF AMERICA

OPM   0 9 8 7 6 5 4 3 2 1

To Jan, who can't be a clown anymore.
Thanks for your friendship and your help.

PROLOGUE

The pressure was there when he woke that morning, a weight on his chest, nothing more. Parker Morgan ignored it. He had too much to do.

Two hours later, as he drove from his breakfast meeting with the department managers of his branch store on Twenty-eighth Street to the downtown store in Grand Rapids, Parker was aware that the pressure was increasing. What was worse, his left arm felt as though it were in a vise.

He didn't want to consider what that could mean.

Hurrying through the employees' entrance of Morgan's Department Store, he greeted Carl, the security guard, and glanced at the time clock on the wall. Nine o'clock. He was late.

"Busy day ahead?" Carl asked.

"As usual," Parker answered, already pushing open the door to the main floor of the two-story department store.

Only personnel from the business offices and a few department managers could be seen, the salesclerks not due for another half hour and customers not let in until ten o'clock. Parker headed for his office, rubbing his left arm and taking in a deep breath.

Damn, but it felt like a cement block was sitting on his chest.

As he entered the office area he expected to see Gene Hill, vice-president and one of the major stock-holders of the Austin-Hill chain of retail stores. Hill was scheduled for a nine o'clock meeting. He'd called last week and set it up.

Parker was pretty sure he knew what Hill wanted to talk about. The Austin-Hill Corporation had made one offer so far to buy Morgan's Department Stores. Parker had been expecting another.

The reception area, however, was empty.

He paused at his secretary's desk. "Gene's not here, yet?"

"He called." Anne Closson handed him his telephone messages. "He's going to be fifteen to twenty minutes late."

"Wish I'd known." Then he wouldn't have driven like a maniac to get to the store on time . . . would have had time to stop and pick up some aspirin. "Do you have anything for pain? Aspirin or ibuprofen?"

"I'm not sure." Anne pulled open her middle desk drawer and glanced over its contents. "Ben has been by twice this morning," she said, pushing things aside in the drawer. "Seems this time there's a problem with a shipment of ties."

Parker had hired Benjamin Waite as an assistant manager with the hopes that the man would take over some of the responsibilities of running a large department store. Instead of easing Parker's job, though, Ben's inability to make decisions was creating problems.

Anne stopped rummaging in the drawer and looked

up. "I don't seem to have anything, but I can get you something. Do you have a headache?"

"Ah . . ." He wasn't sure how to describe what was wrong, only that the pressure on his chest was getting heavier and the vise around his arm tighter. "I think I slept on my arm wrong."

Anne nodded and stood. "I'll find you something. By the way, Loren dropped off the fall window designs for you to okay. I left them on your desk. He'd like an answer this morning, if possible."

"I'll look at them." Parker started for his office. "Bring me whatever you find as soon as you can."

The moment he closed the door to his office, Parker loosened his tie. He didn't want to overreact, but he couldn't seem to get enough air into his lungs. He took in a deep breath, then another.

The pressure on his chest was getting worse. What had started as one block of cement was up to three—or maybe four or five blocks—and the tightening around his arm was becoming unbearable.

Don't panic, he told himself, sitting down in his upholstered chair and trying to relax. It might not be—

Still, he couldn't block out the fact that his father had died of a heart attack. He remembered the day his mother had called, sobbing.

The telephone rang.

A shock of surprise jerked through his body, and Parker stared at the telephone, afraid to answer it. Logic told him it wouldn't be a call telling him he was dead, but the anxiety growing within him was stronger than logic.

Only on the third ring did he reach for the receiver. It was Anne.

"Ben has some aspirin," she said. "He's bringing them."

"Good." Parker wasn't sure, however, that aspirin were going to help.

Relax! he again ordered his body. This was ridiculous. Thirty-three was too young to be worrying about a heart attack. The weight he'd picked up the last few years wasn't all that much, and what was he to do? Eating out four and five times a week didn't help keep the pounds off. And no, he didn't get enough exercise, but who had time with his schedule? Overall, he was healthy.

Of course, everyone had thought his father was healthy and that forty-eight was too young to die.

There was a knock at his door. Parker hoped it was Ben with the aspirin. "Come on in," he called out, and stood.

Benjamin Waite stepped into Parker's office and stopped. Parker stood behind his desk, his right hand pressed against his chest, his eyes wide with fear, his face as white as chalk.

For once in his life, Ben made a decision without hesitation. "Call nine-one-one," he ordered Anne.

ONE

Parker waited until the coffeemaker gurgled its final belch, then filled his mug. Not that he needed any caffeine. In fact, caffeine was one of the things the doctors had told him to eliminate from his life.

Old habits, however, were hard to break.

Such as getting up at the crack of dawn. For years, that had been his routine. He'd work until ten or eleven at night, get to bed by midnight, and be up by five or six. He didn't need an alarm clock; it just happened.

This learning to relax was not an easy task. The alternative, however, was not one he wanted to contemplate.

He sucked in a deep breath. No pain. That was good. He rotated his arm. No pain there, either. All seemed fine.

Coffee mug in hand, he wandered over to the window that faced Gun Lake. The first rays of light were diffused by the mist hanging over the water, and he could barely make out the pontoon boat bobbing up and down at his dock. Waves lapped against the shoreline in a soothing rhythm, while in the distance, a family of ducks called to each other, the sound of their quacking like a cheap comic's laughter.

It wasn't a sound, however, that drew Parker's attention to the yard next door, but a motion. A flowing motion, graceful and elegant. A woman dancing, her body barely more than a silhouette in the dim light.

Fascinated, he watched.

She circled her arms in front of her body, then gave an arced kick with one leg. Her shorts revealed slender, well-toned legs, and her loose-fitting T-shirt didn't fully conceal her womanly curves. Unaware that she had an audience, she faced the lake, only occasionally turning in his direction as she danced.

In the early-morning light, it was impossible for him to make out her features, yet he knew who it was. There was no mistaking the mop of burnished auburn curls that haloed her face. He'd known her when she was a teenager, awkward but never shy. She'd been the first one to greet him the summer his parents bought the cottage at Gun Lake.

Effie Sanders had taught him how to laugh that summer, and for two summers after that. Her sister, Bernadette, had taught him how to love.

Though he'd run into Bern off and on since then, thirteen years had passed since he'd last seen Effie. She'd be twenty-nine now. It didn't seem possible; yet as he watched her floating steps and the graceful arcs and dips of her body, he knew it was true. The gangly awkwardness of her teenage years was gone, replaced by an alluring sensuality apparent in every move she made. At least he found her movements very sensual. Simply watching her was getting a rise out of him.

That was something that hadn't happened for a while. Certainly not since his attack. Even before then, it was usually tall, willowy blondes who sent his blood racing. Sophistication was what he looked for in a bed partner. Class. Not a mystical sprite who danced to unheard music in the early dawn light.

But then again, there had been that one night.

He'd nearly forgotten.

Without hesitation, Parker set down his mug and headed for the back door.

The sky was growing lighter, colors more defined. He closed his screen door quietly, yet it creaked. He knew Effie would have heard, and expected her to stop and turn toward him. Concerned with how he'd changed over the last thirteen years, he sucked in his stomach.

To his disappointment, she continued facing the lake, circling her arms, moving her hands, and kicking her legs. What did come toward him was a small dog. Long-haired and low to the ground, it reminded him of a dust mop his grandmother had used on her floors.

The dog's coat was predominantly brown and gray, with a peppering of white hairs. It wagged its tail in greeting as it trotted toward him, stopped at his feet, and gave a high-pitched bark. Then it hopped about in a circle on its hind legs.

Parker watched, fascinated.

Effie had heard the Morgans' screen door and wasn't surprised by Mopsy's bark of greeting. Mopsy greeted everyone she saw, loved everyone. Which had made her great for the act. As a guard dog, it did have disadvantages.

Not that Effie felt she needed a guard dog this morning. Her intruder was just another vacationer renting the Morgan cottage. Her grandmother had said the place was occupied quite regularly. From Memorial Day to Labor Day, they came, for a weekend, a week, or a month. Couples and families, migrating like the geese, enjoying the lake for a while, then heading back to their homes. With Gun Lake no more than an hour's drive from Grand Rapids, Kalamazoo, and Lansing, it drew a steady flow of visitors. "Summer people," the locals called them. Businesses loved them. The year-round lake people, like her grandparents had been, tolerated them.

Again, Mopsy barked. Afraid her dog might wake others, Effie stopped her workout and turned to face the man. "She wants you to pet her."

He looked up, and Effie gaped, the impact of recognition hitting her hard. "Parker Morgan, is that you?"

Parker grinned as she scanned him from the top of his head to his bare toes, then back to his face. When her mouth broke into a smile, dimples dotting her cheeks, he knew that as much as she'd changed in the last thirteen years, in one way she hadn't. When Effie Sanders smiled, her entire body smiled. Again, he sucked in his stomach. "The one and only."

"I don't believe it!" She started toward him, almost a bounce to her steps. "I didn't think I'd ever see you again. I mean, I've seen you in those TV ads, and you always look so distinguished, but . . ."

She hadn't changed in another way. Effie could still talk a mile a minute. Talk. Laugh. Clown around.

He'd heard she was a clown. He could believe it.

Opening her arms wide, she embraced him. "How the heck are you?"

He hugged her close, inhaling deeply. She smelled good—of sunshine and shampoo, the familiar and the unknown—and he knew he was a heck of a lot better at that moment than he'd been in the last few months. "Not too bad," he lied. "And you?"

"Not too bad." Mentally, Effie kicked herself. For years she'd imagined seeing Parker again. In those scenarios, she'd been warm and friendly, but somewhat aloof. Grown up and sophisticated. The kind of woman a man like Parker Morgan would be interested in . . . would come back to.

So what had she just done? Gone running into his arms like a child.

She stepped back. "It's been a long time."

"Thirteen years."

Thirteen long years, she thought. The first two years she'd been surprised when he didn't show up at the lake during the summer, not even for a weekend. Both summers she'd asked his mother where he was, and Ruth Morgan's answer had been curt and dismissive, though she said it with a polite smile. "He's very busy. His classes at the University of Michigan are demanding, and he's spending his summers at the stores now, learning the business . . . as he should be. My son doesn't have time for play."

That had seemed a shame.

After that, Effie had gone off to college and a life of her own. The Morgans stopped coming to the lake, though her grandmother had said she'd seen Parker on a few rare occasions, but never to talk to. For someone Effie had once known so well, he was now practically a stranger.

Parker patted her on top of her head. "I see you didn't grow any taller, shrimp."

That was enough to remind her they weren't complete strangers. He'd started calling her "shrimp" back when they first met, and the nickname had stuck. She'd loved it, had loved any attention he paid her. He'd teased her, and she'd teased back.

She teased now. "The correct term is vertically challenged. How's the weather up there?"

Smiling, he ruffled her curls. "I think I just ran into

a tornado. Still going around sticking your finger in electric sockets, I see."

"I tried straightening it once. It was too much hassle. I'm afraid I'm stuck with curls."

Again, he touched her hair, this time wrapping a strand around a finger. "I always thought you had beautiful hair."

Parker let the curl slide over his fingertip. His comment had sounded like a line. He wasn't quite sure how to act with Effie, what to say. Up until that one night on the dock, she'd always been the younger sister, the one he teased and laughed with.

Back then, he really hadn't noticed the gold flecks in the green of her eyes. Hadn't been aware of how delicate and cute her nose was or how, when she wasn't smiling, her mouth had a slight pout that was very sexy. She'd turned into an alluring woman, who was teasing him simply with her presence.

He sucked in his stomach once more.

She immediately glanced down, and he realized all he'd done was call her attention to his potbelly. Giving up, he let the muscles relax. "Pretty bad, isn't it? I have lost twenty pounds in the last two months."

"Some woman feeding you too much?" The moment she asked, Effie wished she hadn't. Who was or wasn't feeding him was none of her business. They weren't even friends. Friends kept in touch. Friends didn't kiss and run.

He chuckled. "Who has time for a woman? My problem's been too many meals at restaurants and fast-food outlets." He glanced down at her left hand. "What about you? Is there a man in your life?"

"Not anymore."

"Meaning?"

She shrugged, not wanting to go into it. She was

getting used to being let down by men, if a person could get used to that.

"Divorced?" he asked.

"No. You have to get married to get divorced. I've never gotten that far. I guess I clown around too much."

"Isn't that what clowns are supposed to do?" His gaze traveled down her body. "Not that I can picture you as a clown. Not with your figure. You do that dancing every day?"

"Dancing?"

He looked toward the water and motioned with his hands, and she understood. "You mean the tai chi. I only started this year. I didn't think anyone would be up this early. Usually I do it in private, but I thought it would be fun to do it out here."

"Tai chi?"

"Tai chi chuan, to be exact." She spelled it for him. "It's an old Chinese form of martial arts and a study of inner harmony and fitness. I like the way it relaxes me and gives me energy at the same time. It—"

She stopped herself. She was going on like a salesperson making a pitch, chattering away like the parrot she and her partner had at the party store. "It's fun," she finished.

He nodded. "Sounds like I should try it. That's what I'm supposed to be doing here—relaxing."

"Well, the tai chi will do it." She wasn't sure what else to say, and he said nothing. Effie was rarely at a loss for words, but then, she rarely ever acted normal around Parker Morgan. From the first time she'd met him, he'd taken her breath away. As a teenager, he'd been gorgeous, all muscular and tan, with thick brown hair and vibrant blue eyes. A real heartthrob.

He still took her breath away. Maybe his body wasn't as well toned or tanned as it once had been, and maybe there were a few gray hairs at his temples and tiny lines at the corners of his eyes, but the guy was still a hunk. One very distinguished-looking hunk.

A high-pitched bark near her feet took care of what to say. Effie looked down and laughed. "I may not be married, but I do have a child . . . at least she thinks she's my baby. Parker, meet Mopsy."

Mopsy wagged her brushlike tail and lifted a tiny paw. Kneeling, Parker shook her paw. "Glad to meet you, Miss Mopsy. I see you didn't inherit your mother's curls or red hair." He glanced up at Effie. "What is she, anyway?"

"Part shih tzu, they said at the shelter. Part traveling man."

The dog was wagging her tail, her bright button eyes communicating her adoration and her tongue lolling out the side of her mouth. Parker laughed and rose to his feet. "She's adorable. Just like her mother."

"Yeah, right. Adorable."

He had a feeling he hadn't said the right thing. "You always made me laugh."

"That's Effie, always good for a laugh." The mockery was clear in her tone. "Not that it wasn't a challenge with you. You and your parents were good training for me. I've never met such a serious family. I know I drove your mother crazy, and your dad—"

Effie stopped, immediately growing serious. "I heard he died. I'm sorry."

"It was a shock." But then, as Parker had learned, death always was . . . and near-death experiences. "I understand your grandmother died just recently."

Effie nodded. "That's why I'm here. We're getting the cottage ready to sell."

He glanced toward the small, aluminum-sided cottage. It was half the size of the one he'd stepped out of. "You're not going to keep it?"

"No, we decided we really couldn't afford to, not with me living in Kalamazoo and Bern in Chicago. Also, after Grandpa died, the place really got run-down. It would cost too much to fix it up just to rent in the summer."

She kept talking, and Parker found himself staring at her mouth, memories of that night thirteen years ago racing back. How he'd forgotten, he didn't know. Maybe because, when he'd kissed her that night, she'd been only sixteen—jailbait—and he'd wanted to forget. Or maybe because that night had been crazy.

"Bern's coming," she said, and he pulled his thoughts back to the present. "Sometime this afternoon. She couldn't get away until then. She said she saw you at a trade show recently. What did you think?"

"Think?" He thought she wasn't jailbait anymore.

Effie used her hands to outline the contour of a female body. "She looked pretty good, didn't she?"

"She?" He finally realized Effie meant her sister. "Oh, yeah."

Her laughter bubbled. "I still remember the first time you saw her. Boy, did your eyes bug out."

"You exaggerate, as usual."

"Do not. I remember exactly what happened." She pointed toward his dock, the mist over the water now rising and his pontoon boat visible. "You were showing me your boat—actually, your dad's boat—and all at once you stopped talking and just stared over my head toward our cottage. If your eyes weren't bugging out, I don't know what you'd call it."

He smiled, remembering. Effie probably was right. Bernadette did have that effect on men. "So? I imagine a few men have gone buggy-eyed over you."

"Oh, sure. All the time." Again, she laughed, but she shook her head. "Let's face it, Parker, men just don't react to me as they do to Bern. It's hard to beat a beautiful face, blond hair, blue eyes, and long legs. Plus she's sophisticated and poised. Mature and responsible. I'm—" Effie fanned her hands in the air. "Well, I'm not any of those things."

He didn't completely agree, and what she lacked in sophistication, she made up for in other ways. "That hair of yours is an eye-catcher on its own."

"I catch their eye, then usually lose it when I start clowning around. Will you still be at the lake this afternoon?"

"I'll still be here. I'm supposed to be here for two weeks."

"Really?"

"Really." From her grin, Parker knew Effie had something up her sleeve. He was certain it wouldn't take him long to discover her plan. Effie had never been good at keeping secrets.

She continued grinning. "Bern will be glad to see you. I think she broke up with her latest boyfriend."

"Did she? That's too bad." Not that he was surprised. The night he'd had dinner with Bernadette, she'd complained about the man she was seeing . . . and about her job.

"She was asking about you just the other day," Effie went on.

"Was she now?" He saw the matchmaking coming. It was time to change the subject. "You going to need any help?" He nodded toward her grandparents' cottage.

She also looked that way, the laughter once again leaving her face. "I don't think so. Until Bern arrives and we can decide together what to keep and what to toss, I'm just going to go through Grandma's photo albums. Which means, I'm probably going to do a lot of crying."

"For you, it's got to be like losing your mother."

She nodded. "From the time I was five, Grandma *was* my mother." Her gaze drifted back to the cottage. "And Grandpa was my father. Oh, Dad did make his occasional visits, and there was that one time he decided to be a parent and took us with him." Effie shook her head. "That was a fiasco. He might think digging through sand, looking for things people buried centuries ago, is fun, but I sure was happy to get back here."

"Your father still in Egypt?"

"Yes. He did come for Grandma's funeral, but the next day he was on his way back to the dig. Howard Sanders, the Mummy Man."

"And his daughter, Effie the Clown."

"Not anymore." She knelt and scooped up Mopsy. The little dog licked her chin, and Effie absently petted her. "Now I'm just your average businesswoman. The rate I'm going, I'll soon be sedate enough for your mother to approve of."

"My mother moved to San Diego two years ago to live with her sister," he said. "I wouldn't worry about her approval."

Effie wondered if he would ever understand how much she had wanted his mother's approval . . . and his. She was glad he didn't know how madly in love she'd been with him thirteen years ago.

A silly crush.

Adolescent.

Bernadette was his type, always had been and always would be. For men like Parker Morgan, Effie Sanders was the shrimpy little sister they patted on the head. The one who made them laugh. The clown.

Except, she could no longer be the clown.

"I guess I'd better go on in and feed Mopsy," she said, afraid she was going to get maudlin if she didn't leave.

Parker glanced at his watch. "Guess I'd better get a move on too. This morning, I'm supposed to play golf with some guys I met yesterday."

"Do stop by this afternoon," Effie said as she turned to leave. "When Bern's here."

"What do you think? Is it providence?" Effie asked, sitting on the floor beside her dog. Mopsy merely wagged her tail as she gobbled up the food in her dish.

It certainly seemed like it, Effie mused. Only the week before, when she'd called Bernadette to set up a time when they could both be at the cottage, Bern had mentioned Parker. "Wouldn't it be something if he were there?" she'd said.

"Don't hold your breath," Effie had told her. "Grandma said she hadn't seen him at the lake more than a dozen times in the last five years."

"I never should have broken up with him." Her sigh had carried across the lines. "God, I'm tired of the men around here. They're all a bunch of phonies."

Effie had known then that Bern had broken up with her latest heartthrob. One more perfect male who'd shown a flaw. Not that Effie was going to say anything. Her love life wasn't going any better. "So you can take a week or two off?"

"It's not a matter of can I. I *will* take two weeks off," Bern had said firmly. "I'm tired of being told how important I am, then being denied a raise or a step up the ladder. I'm tired of this city, its crime rate and high cost of living. I'm getting away for a while, and if they don't like it, they can lump it."

Bernadette's attitude was certainly a change from five years earlier, when she'd asserted that Chicago was the only place to live and the Fashion Mannequin was the only place to work. "Wouldn't it be something," Effie said to Mopsy, stroking the dog's long coat, "if Bern and Parker ended up together."

It wasn't beyond the realm of possibilities. For three summers, from the time Bernadette had been fifteen until she was eighteen, Parker and she had been a twosome. Oh, they'd taken Effie with them sometimes when they went out, especially when Grandma had ordered them to, but she'd always been the outsider, the little sister to be tolerated and ignored. Neither had ever guessed how she felt about Parker, and Effie knew that was just as well. They would only have laughed.

"Can you imagine?" she asked her dog. "Me with him?"

The idea made her smile. She'd dreamed about it more than once, back when she was sixteen. In her daydreams, she'd pictured him coming to her and saying, "I don't know what I ever saw in Bern. It's you I want."

But it had only been a dream.

His mother had said it quite plainly when Effie had asked why Parker hadn't come back to the lake. "Why does it matter? He wouldn't be interested in you, my dear. You don't have the . . . the . . ."

Effie still remembered how Ruth Morgan had groped for the word and how it had hurt when she'd found it.

"Class," she'd said, and had smiled politely, as she always did. "You don't have the *class* my son needs."

"I have all the class anyone needs," Effie had told

the woman. She'd put on a show that afternoon, sticking her nose in the air and turning her back on Ruth Morgan before marching away. But the word had hurt. Deep down it had stuck like a burr, always there, scratching away at her self-confidence.

Even when people complimented her on her skills as a clown, the word had hung in the back of her head. Clowns didn't have class. Clowns were the jokers, the fools.

Only fools wanted what they could never have.

Mopsy finished her food and climbed onto Effie's lap. Lost in thought, Effie continued stroking her dog, remembering. The feelings and emotions from all those years ago were coming back. The frustration and longing.

There had been that one time, that one night.

That night she'd thought she might have a chance. It had seemed like one of her daydreams come true, at least to a point. Afterward, she'd pushed that memory to the back of her mind, along with so many other ones. But as she stared at her grandmother's kitchen wall, the memory came back.

The moon had been full that night, illuminating the lake like a heavenly spotlight. She'd been too restless to watch television with her grandparents and had gone outside. She'd been sitting on the edge of the dock, dangling her feet in the water, when Parker joined her.

She knew he'd had a fight with Bernadette. Bern had told her she'd dumped him, then she'd gone off to a movie with her girlfriend Cindy. So Effie wasn't surprised when Parker sat down beside her and sighed. More than once he'd come to her for advice when he and Bern had a fight.

But that night had been different. That night he'd talked about his parents, their plans for him, and his confusion. That night she'd heard rebellion in his words. Rebellion and anger.

That night, he'd kissed her.

She hadn't expected it, and she hadn't been sure how to react. He'd been twenty; a man, in her opinion. She'd just turned sixteen, and her experiences with boys had been limited.

A part of her had felt guilty about kissing her sister's boyfriend—ex or not—while another part had loved every minute. Only when he'd pushed her down on the dock and begun groping under her shirt, touching her breasts and making her feel all funny inside, had she gotten scared and pulled back. Shaken, they'd both stared at each other in disbelief. Then he'd mumbled something and left.

That was the last time she'd seen him in person.

Until today.

"What he did that night didn't mean anything," Effie told Mopsy. "He was upset with Bernadette, and I was just conveniently there."

She'd told herself that a thousand times and knew it was true. If it had meant something, he would have contacted her. If it had meant . . .

"It didn't mean a thing. Not one damn thing," she said harshly, and put Mopsy back on the floor. Standing, Effie brushed away the memories. "Time for me to get to work."

Parker stroked the ball gently and held his breath as it rolled toward the cup. For a moment it hung on the edge, teetering . . . then it fell.

"Good putt," his partner said, and marked their scorecard. Together they joined the other two in their foursome.

Parker had only met these three men the day before, but it didn't matter. They were all up at the lake and on the golf course for the same reason: to relax, to forget work for a few hours, and get a little fresh air and exercise. Not that work was completely forgotten.

"What's so difficult nowadays is finding good help," Bill, the tallest of the three said, pulling out his three wood as he gauged the distance to the next green.

"I know what you mean," Parker said. "I thought I'd hired a man who could take some of the load off my shoulders, but it turns out he can't make decisions on his own. Instead of easing my job, he's added to it."

"So fire him and get someone else," Tom, the oldest man there, said.

Parker had considered it. "I hate to fire him. He is a good idea man. Also, it's not that easy to fire someone. I heard one store owner say it's as difficult as getting rid of a wife."

"Tell me about that." Dave, Parker's partner for the day, rolled his eyes. "Don't ask me what my divorce cost. I'm still paying."

Bill paused on his way to the tee. "They say, 'Behind every successful man is a good woman.' I've found most successful men are either divorced or on wife number two or three. What about you, Parker?" he asked, looking his way. "How many times have you been married?"

"Never have had time to get married," he said, and smiled. "Sounds like I lucked out."

Tom shook his head. "Not necessarily. I've been married for twenty years, and to the same woman, no less. I consider myself relatively successful, and I can't imagine not being married to Kate. She keeps me sane, makes me laugh. Without her, I think life would have driven me crazy years ago."

"So you're the exception," Bill said, and placed his ball on the tee.

They were quiet as he teed off, but Parker smiled again. There was one woman who'd always made him laugh, but he doubted Effie Sanders would keep him sane. Just looking at her that morning had made him a little crazy.

TWO

Effie sat on the faded rose-patterned carpet in the living room, albums of photographs spread about her and Mopsy curled up by her side. She hadn't meant to spend so much time going through the pictures, but each held memories, each a measure of the passing of time. A towhead and a carrottop had gone from toddlers to grown women; their grandparents from salt-and-pepper hair to white.

Only occasionally did Effie find a picture of her parents. She barely remembered her mother, who had died when she was five, and after turning his children over to his parents to raise, her father had become a near nonentity. Most of the time he was away, off at a dig or giving lectures. Off satisfying his needs, but not the needs of his daughters.

"Obviously, I learned well from him," Effie muttered, and rose to her feet, leaving the albums on the floor. Mopsy jumped up and followed her.

"Hungry?" she asked, and dropped a dog biscuit into Mopsy's dish. Finding something for herself wasn't as easy.

The refrigerator was empty, and the only thing in the cupboards that looked appetizing was a can of soup. It had been a year since her grandmother had had her first stroke. Effie had come up then, packed up the necessities, and had moved her grandmother down to Kalamazoo, to live with her. They'd hoped she would recover enough to return to the cottage, but that had never happened. Ethel Sanders's time had run out on the night of March twenty-sixth.

Thirty minutes later, the soup heated and eaten, Effie left a note for Bernadette, closed the door on a dejected-looking Mopsy, and headed for the grocery store.

Parker saw Effie the moment he pushed his cart around the corner and started down the canned-goods aisle. Her leap to reach a can on the top shelf would have impressed Michael Jordan. It was the grin on her face that amused Parker. She might be twenty-nine, all woman, and very attractive, but she still had that ability to laugh at life.

Appreciatively, he applauded.

Effie turned, her grin growing broader when she saw him. "Ah, a man of height, just what I need."

He pushed his cart next to hers and looked at the cans high above her head. "So what are you after, shrimp?"

She wrinkled her nose at his use of the old nickname and pointed at a group of cans. "Those black-eyed peas. Why is it what you don't want is easy to get, and what you do want is always on the top shelf?"

"It's a conspiracy."

"Most definitely." She nodded, her generous mouth once again forming a delightful pout. "All you tall people stay up late at night devising ways to make life for short people more difficult: kitchen cupboards you can't reach, chairs where your feet don't touch, and worst of all—" She waved a hand toward the shelves, her slender fingers pointing the way. "This."

He reached for the cans of black-eyed peas. "How many do you want?"

"Two. I tried using stilts in a grocery store once," she said, and wobbled her body from side to side, wildly yet gracefully sweeping her hands about and barely missing the cans on the lower shelves. "I proved that theory of 'what goes up must come down.' I also discovered grocers get very upset when you wipe out an entire display."

Parker laughed. He could picture everything—her on stilts, weaving through a grocery store, losing her balance, and falling. He could also imagine the manager's anger. "I don't believe you."

Her expression totally serious, she crossed her heart. "Honest truth. Not that it was *all* my fault. I still contend that floors shouldn't be waxed that much."

"You're as crazy as ever." And he was glad. "Remember that time you decided to pick peaches using stilts?"

"The stilts I made out of two-by-four scraps? Oh yes. I also remember how upset Bern was when I fell on top of her and got her white slacks dirty. She hadn't wanted me along in the first place." Mischievously, Effie grinned at him. "And neither had you."

"Not so. I always enjoyed having you around. You made us laugh."

"I don't think laughing was what you had in mind for that afternoon. Which is why Grandma insisted I go along."

He'd suspected as much. "Your grandmother was one smart lady."

"Very."

Effie glanced away, and the laughter disappeared. Her expression was somber when she looked back. "How did your golf game go this morning?"

"Good . . . fine." He mentally kicked himself for mentioning her grandmother again. The loss was clearly still bothering her. "I played at Orchard Hills. It's not a bad course. Have you ever played there?"

She shook her head. "I don't play golf that much. People take the game too seriously. I did learn, though. There was this guy I was dating . . ." The laughter was back. "He taught me all about stroking the ball, getting it into the hole, and follow-through."

Parker lifted his eyebrows. "Are we still discussing golf?"

"Why, of course."

Effie kept her expression totally innocent, but her thoughts weren't. How could they be innocent when the man standing in front of her was so tempting? His blue eyes, the deep rumble of his laughter . . . just the way he looked in a golf shirt and shorts turned her on. When he'd put the two cans of black-eyed peas in her cart, she'd tried not to stare at his arms and wonder how they would feel wrapped around her.

To think such foolish thoughts was a waste of time.

She knew the realities of life. Parker might joke with her, but Bernadette was his kind of woman. They had the same interests, the same drive. Once Bern arrived, Parker would only have eyes for her. It had always been that way, and always would be. So why fight the inevitable? What she should be doing was helping her sister.

"What are you doing for dinner tonight?" she asked.

Parker hesitated. "Dinner?"

She hadn't thought of it before, but it would work. "Why don't you have dinner with Bern and me? It would give us a chance to catch up on old times."

"Dinner with the Sanders sisters." He grinned. "Sounds good to me. What time?"

"Six-thirty? Seven?" Effie already had a plan. Before dinner was over, she would find an excuse to leave. Bern certainly wouldn't object. She'd already indicated an interest in renewing her relationship with Parker.

"I don't believe it," a female voice called out from the far end of the aisle. "Have I gone back in time? Effie? Parker? Are the two of you really here?"

Effie recognized the voice, but not the woman coming toward them. She tried not to stare, but she couldn't believe how much Cindy Nelson had changed.

While growing up, Cindy and Bernadette had been like two peas in a pod. Bern was the taller of the two, but in high school, they'd both been blond, model thin, and always picture-perfect. The last time Effie had seen Cindy was at Cindy's wedding, when Bern had stood up with her as her maid of honor. That had been ten years ago. Since then, Cindy had picked up at least fifty pounds, her hair was now a mousy brown, and the only makeup she was wearing was a too red lipstick.

"Isn't this crazy," Cindy said to Parker as she neared. "I don't see you for a lifetime, and then I run into you twice in two months. But then again, for as many years as I lived in Grand Rapids, I'm surprised I didn't run into you before, especially considering how many times I've been in your store. I must say, you're looking a heck of a lot better this time."

"Feeling better too," Parker said, moving his cart to give Cindy room. "What about you? How are you doing?"

"Surviving," she said with a sigh, and glanced Effie's

way. "You're looking great. I was sorry to hear about your grandmother."

"It was a shock."

"She was a wonderful woman. I wanted to go to the funeral, but I couldn't. I'd hoped to see Bern again. When Dale and I were breaking up, I was on the phone to her all the time, but lately . . ." She sighed again. "It's been ages."

"She's coming up here, to the lake," Effie said. "She may even be here by now. You two will have to get together."

"Tell her to call me. My daughter Mandy and I have moved in with my parents. Mom watches her at night while I'm at work, and during the day when I'm sleeping. The condition Mandy's in, I don't dare leave her with anyone else." Cindy pointed toward the end of the store where the pharmacy was located. "I'm here to get another prescription filled."

Effie knew, from what Bernadette had told her, that Cindy's daughter had been born with several medical problems, including a defective urinary tract and kidneys. Bern hadn't gone into great detail, other than to say that Cindy had spent so much time with the baby, her husband, Dale, had finally left her. That had been at least six years ago. Parker seemed more up-to-date on Mandy's condition. "Is she going to have that operation?" he asked.

Cindy shook her head. "We tried scheduling one, but she put up such a fuss, we canceled. The doctors are saying, with her present attitude, Mandy's chances of survival wouldn't be good. All we're doing is keeping things controlled with medication. I just—"

She paused, taking in a deep breath and blinking back tears. Effie felt she should say something, but Parker spoke first. "Is there anything I can do?"

"Not unless you can talk her into having that operation. I need a magician or a—" Cindy looked at Effie. "I'd forgotten. You're a clown."

"Not anymore."

Cindy ignored that comment. "Mandy loves clowns. She's just like you were when you were little, Effie. She has pictures of clowns on her bedroom walls, clown dolls, clown books, clown everything. If you could come see her sometime, dressed as a clown, well, she would love it."

It pained her, but Effie said it again. "I'm not doing that anymore."

"But you still have the outfit, don't you?" There was an element of desperation in the question. "I know it probably wouldn't make any difference, but if you did come by and you talked to her, encouraged her to have the operation, well, maybe—"

Cindy stopped, the tears that had been welling in her eyes spilling over onto her cheeks. She pulled a tissue from her pocket and dabbed at her face. "I'm sorry. I shouldn't bother you with my problems. It's just that I don't know what to do. All of this is my fault. She's had so many complications and been in so much pain after her operations, that when the doctors assured me the last operation would take care of her problem, I told Mandy there'd be no more. I promised her there would be no more until the kidney transplant. Now . . ."

Effie understood. Some promises shouldn't be made.

Parker put an arm around Cindy's shoulders and drew her close. Effie could hear his comforting murmurs. He was giving Cindy the support she needed.

All she did was let people down.

Four months earlier, she wouldn't have said no. She would have willingly donned her baggy trousers and shirt, put on her oversized shoes and makeup, and gathered up Mopsy to go see Mandy. It had been so easy then.

Now it was impossible.

Sniffling back her tears, Cindy gave one last wipe at her eyes and took in a deep breath. Then she looked up at Parker. "Here I am going on about Mandy. What about you? How are you doing after your heart attack?"

"Heart attack?" Effie repeated, certain she hadn't heard right.

"You can imagine my surprise," Cindy said to her. "There I was, walking back to Mandy's room from the cafeteria, and who do they wheel by but Parker."

"It wasn't a heart attack," he said, wanting to erase the worry from Effie's face. "When I saw Cindy, I was coming back from a test, and we still thought I'd had a heart attack. I mean, I had all the symptoms—the pressure on the chest, the tightening around the arm, the difficulty in breathing. But when all the test results were in, they showed I hadn't had one. It doesn't sound as dramatic, but as far as the doctors can tell, what I had was a stress attack."

"A stress attack?" Stepping back, Cindy looked at him, then shook her head. "That was more than a stress attack." She turned to Effie. "When I saw him, he looked terrible."

"I was still in pain," he explained. "Now if I have an attack, I use the nitroglycerin nose spray, and I'm better in seconds."

"You needed nitroglycerin?" Effie asked.

"Not that often. Not for a month now."

Effie didn't look satisfied. "Exactly what did the doctors tell you?"

"That my body is giving me a warning. I'm fine. Really," Parker insisted, and realized he did feel fine. Curiously aroused around Effie, but definitely fine. "I think the doctors were right. All I need to do is watch my diet, exercise, and take a vacation."

"The tai chi I do would probably help you."

He wasn't sure if tai chi would help. It depended on the instructor, and he had his preferences. "Are you offering to teach me?"

"Me?"

"You could show me a few moves, let me see if I like it."

"I . . . I'm really not competent to teach someone else. I'm still a novice."

She was shaking her head. He pushed. "But you say it's relaxing?"

"Yes. I mean, sort of."

She didn't look relaxed, and watching her that morning hadn't been relaxing . . . not for him. From the moment he'd spotted her, he'd been half-aroused. A man concerned with improving his health probably shouldn't have the urge to make love with a woman, but he was glad to know the impulse was still there. He certainly hadn't experienced the desire for the last few months. If stroking a ball, putting it in the hole, and following through had been part of Effie's experience in learning golf, what could he expect with a lesson in tai chi?

How much body contact would there be?

He was game to find out. "I'm not looking for an expert. Just an idea if it's something I'd like to try. How about showing me some of the moves this afternoon?"

"I, ah—" Effie glanced at her watch. "I have to run over to Shelbyville and put an ad in next week's *Penasee Globe*. We're having a yard sale next weekend."

"That shouldn't take you long. What? A half hour?"

"Bern should be at the cottage when I get back."

He could tell Effie was groping for excuses. He didn't let her off. "You can show both of us."

"But—"

Cindy broke in before Effie came up with another excuse. "What time did you say Bern was coming?"

Parker decided that was his cue to leave. "I'll see you in a half hour, then," he said to Effie, and nodded at Cindy. "Good to see you again. I'll try to get by and see Mandy."

"Do," Cindy said eagerly. "She'd like that."

He pushed his cart away before Effie could speak, and as he rounded the end of the aisle, he heard Cindy ask Effie again when she expected Bernadette. Parker found it interesting that he didn't care. Seeing Bernadette again would be nice, but nothing more. Seeing her six months ago in Chicago had been nice. She'd been as beautiful as ever, elegantly dressed and in total control. They'd gone out to dinner and had talked about old times and new, mostly complaining about the uncertainties of the retail business. He'd even kissed her good night.

It hadn't excited him.

What did excite him was the idea of spending time with Effie, being close to her, hearing her voice and her laughter. Ever since that morning, he'd felt a new energy in his body. For the first time in weeks he wasn't worrying about the pressure in his chest returning, and was actually almost ready to admit that this relaxing might not be so bad after all.

Glancing down at the front of his shorts, he realized he wasn't exactly relaxed. He wondered what Effie would say if she knew the effect she was having on him. She'd had a crush on him once. He'd known it even before Bernadette had told him. But that had been years ago, back when Effie was only sixteen. She was a woman now.

And he was a man.

Whistling, he pushed his cart toward the checkout stand.

Effie was certain Bernadette would be at the cottage by the time she finished her grocery shopping and made her stops. It bothered her when she neared the cottage and could see the only car there was her grandparents' old Buick. A grocery bag in each arm, she headed for the back door.

A note was stuck between the screen door and the jamb. She pulled it out with her teeth, then managed to open the screen door and back door with only her fingertips. Mopsy eagerly greeted her, and Effie let the dog out. Not until she'd set the bags on the kitchen table was she able to read the note.

It wasn't from Bern.

Problem at the store. Had to run into G.R. Be back by seven, was scrawled in pencil on the half sheet of typing paper. He'd signed with a large *P*.

Not having to show Parker tai chi moves—even if it might help him relax—was a relief. The man oozed far too much sex appeal for her sanity. Being around him had her as jumpy as a clown on a trampoline. Now she was the one who could relax.

He would be back in time for dinner. Bern would be there, and that would be that. Parker Morgan wouldn't be throwing sexual innuendos Effie Sanders's way. Not after he saw Bern again.

But where was Bernadette?

The blinking red light on the answering machine caught her attention, and Effie walked over to the telephone and pushed the message button. Bernadette's voice sounded rushed and was tinged with exasperation. Her message paralleled Parker's. She couldn't get away because of problems at the store. Unlike Parker, Bernadette wouldn't be arriving by seven. She wouldn't be arriving at all that day. "See you tomorrow," she said before clicking off.

So much for providence and well-laid plans.

Effie looked at the grocery bags on the table. After Parker had left, she and Cindy had worked out the perfect plan. Cindy would call at seven-fifteen. Effie would answer the telephone, would tell Bern and Parker that she had to go somewhere, and then she would take off, not to return until the lovebirds had had time to rekindle the flame.

Everything had sounded so simple an hour ago.

Effie knew the moment Parker arrived. Mopsy's excited barks alerted her even before his soft knock on the back door. Wiping the tears from her cheeks, she hoped her eyes didn't look as red as they felt. How those heroines in the movies always looked so beautiful after a good cry was beyond her. She always resembled a ghoul from a horror show.

"Bernadette's not here," Effie said as she neared the screen door. "I called your store and left a message."

Parker shook his head. "I didn't get any message."

"She's still in Chicago. There were problems at her store too."

"I'm sorry to hear that," he said, but he didn't sound sorry. Smiling, he held up a bottle of wine. "I brought this."

"I didn't—" She stopped herself. He was here for a dinner she hadn't prepared. Crying over old photographs, she hadn't even thought about dinner. But that didn't matter. It didn't even matter that the reason she'd invited him was to get him together with Bernadette. She'd made the invitation and now she needed to come up with a meal, and fast.

Mopsy continued barking, going through her dance routine, bouncing about on her hind legs in front of the screen door. "Quiet," Effie ordered, and scooped up the dog before pushing open the screen. "Come on in. I was just about to get things started."

Parker stepped into the cottage and stopped in front of her. "You haven't started dinner?"

"Well . . ." She couldn't very well lie. All he had to do was look into the kitchen and he would see she hadn't. "I, ah, got busy looking at pictures and forgot the time."

He glanced toward the living room, where the albums and pictures still lay on the carpet. "Having a rough time saying good-bye?"

She nodded, afraid to trust her voice, and turned toward the kitchen. His hand on her shoulder stopped her. "I've got an idea," he said. "Instead of you cooking, let's go to Sam's Joint. It's been years since I've been there."

Years for her, too, and she'd always loved the barbecued ribs at Sam's. It would be good to get out of the cottage for a while. Too many memories lay inside these walls.

It would also be safer. The touch of Parker's hand on her shoulder had sent shivers down her spine, and the way her thoughts had been running that day, she didn't trust herself alone with him.

Stepping away, she glanced at his tan sport shirt, brown slacks, and brown loafers. He looked like one of the models in the ads for his store. Her cutoffs and skimpy halter top didn't compare, and she had to do something about her eyes. A few cold compresses might help. "Let me go change."

His gaze traveled down the front of her, then back, settling at her cleavage, the curves of her breasts prominently displayed. Slowly, he grinned. "You look fine to me."

"Spoken like a true male." She laughed, but her thoughts once again took off, flying back to memories of that night on the dock and his kisses. A tingle of anticipation ran through her body, then she remembered her sister. Seducing Parker—if she even could—was no way to act. The idea was to get him together with Bern.

Carrying Mopsy with her, Effie headed for her bedroom. "I'll change."

Parker followed her as far as the living room. There he stopped and glanced around. How clearly he remembered the hours he'd spent in that room, waiting for Bernadette to get ready. Effie's grandfather would ask him about the weather, her grandmother would ask about his family, then they would go back to watching whatever was on the television. It was Effie who would entertain him, telling him jokes or showing him the latest trick she'd learned.

Mopsy came trotting in, sniffing at his pant legs. He scooped up the dog, amazed by how little it weighed. Stroking Mopsy's long hair, he stepped into the living room, heading for the photo albums on the floor. A picture scrunched into a wad caught his interest. Curious, he picked it up and carefully straightened it out.

"You resolve your problem at the store?" Effie called from the bedroom.

"As far as I could."

Frowning, he stared at the picture of a clown. Looking back at him was a white face, painted smile, and bulbous red nose. The hair was red, but not curly, and a baggy shirt and pants, both covered with sequins, disguised the wearer's figure. Nevertheless, he knew it was Effie. Her eyes gave her away. Like emeralds, they brightened her face. And if he'd had any doubts, the dog poking its head out of one of the clown's oversized pockets erased them. It was Mopsy.

Parker called back to Effie. "When did you actually become a clown?"

She didn't answer right away, and he was beginning to think she hadn't heard him, when she finally spoke. "The year after I graduated from college. Hey, I hear Morgan's may be coming to Kalamazoo."

"It's being discussed." As well as other options. "You told Cindy you weren't a clown anymore. Wasn't it as much fun as you thought it would be?"

"It, ah—it was fun."

Her answer was strained, and she sounded closer. He turned to find her standing in the doorway to her room, buttoning a gold silk blouse. She'd changed to jeans, but her feet were bare and her blouse wasn't tucked in. She looked sexier than when she'd had on the shorts and halter top, and he found himself staring at the button she was buttoning. Realizing where he was looking, he jerked his gaze up to her face.

The look in her eyes mirrored his, and he knew they were no longer facing each other as mere friends. The air between them was charged with awareness, and whether the timing was right or wrong, he wanted one thing—to make love with Effie Sanders.

She was the one who broke eye contact. Turning, she went back into her bedroom. "I'll only be a minute or two more," she said, a huskiness to her voice that hadn't been there before.

"Take your time," he called back, knowing he needed time himself to come to terms with his feelings.

The telephone rang in the kitchen, the sound startling him. He jerked his head in that direction, then asked Effie if he should get it.

"Could you?"

Effie didn't think about Cindy until the words were out of her mouth. Then she looked at the clock. It was exactly seven-fifteen.

She'd called Parker at his store, leaving the message for him, but she'd forgotten to call Cindy and tell her that Bern wouldn't be coming and the plan was off.

One sandal on and one in her hand, Effie hurried to the kitchen. Parker glanced her way, smiled, and held the receiver out to her. "Cindy wants to talk to you."

"I thought it was you answering the phone," Cindy said after Effie warily said hello. "How was I to know *he* would answer?"

"And?" Effie kept her gaze on Parker. From his grin, she knew Cindy had told all.

"And I said, 'This is your escape call. Get out of there and leave the lovebirds alone.' "

"Oh." She wasn't sure what else to say. "Well, I guess, ah . . . I'll have Bern call you tomorrow."

As soon as she hung up the telephone, Effie started back to her bedroom. "I'll be ready in a minute," she said without turning, afraid to face Parker.

"Take your time," he said, and she knew he was following her. "Want to explain that call?"

She kept her gaze forward. "No."

He chuckled, the warm rumble sending a rush of delight to her stomach, and she knew she was in trouble. Deep trouble.

"You had it all planned, didn't you?" he asked, far too close for her comfort.

She continued into her bedroom, needing distance between them. "I thought you and Bern would want some time alone."

"So you were going to duck out on us. Except Bern isn't here, and now you're stuck with me."

He'd followed her into her bedroom, and Effie knew she couldn't keep running. Facing him, she lifted her chin, ready to joke about the situation. Only his smile made her legs weak, and the look in his eyes was so warm, she couldn't think of any jokes, couldn't think of anything but how enticing his mouth looked.

She held her breath when he touched her face, the backs of his fingers brushing over her cheek. His gaze drifted to her lips, and she automatically licked them, waiting . . . never looking away.

He touched her mouth with the tip of his index finger, grazing her lips and teasing her insides. "Hungry?" he asked.

Yes, her mind cried. Hungry for him, for his touch and his kisses.

He smiled. "I know I am."

Abruptly, he turned and started back to the living room. "If we don't get a move on, we'll never get a table."

THREE

Hungry?

As Parker drove them to the north side of the lake, Effie played his question over in her head. She was hungry all right, for something she couldn't have.

Effie Sanders and Parker Morgan together?

What a laugh.

She glanced his way, needing a reality check. It was one thing to dream about being loved by a man like Parker, another to believe it could happen. She was through setting herself up for disappointments. Experience should have taught her something by now.

Parker turned his head, looking at her, and his smile chased away all reality. "We'll probably have to wait for a table, you know," he said.

"I know."

His attention returned to the road, but she continued watching him. Why couldn't she push these silly feelings away? So he'd smiled. Big deal. A lot of men smiled at her.

Of course, their smiles didn't twist her stomach into knots and take her breath away.

She didn't understand what was going on. In her years of being a clown, she'd learned to read body language. Parker's was confusing her. One minute she got the feeling he was attracted to her, the next he was pulling back.

Dang you, Bern, for not showing up, Effie silently cursed. How could she even think about Parker in a romantic way when her sister was interested?

"Bernadette surprised me the other day," Effie said, needing to put the situation into perspective. "She said she was really sorry she ever broke up with you."

"Broke up with me?" Parker glanced at her again, his dark brows lifting and a slight smile touching his lips. "I was under the impression I broke up with her."

"Really?" That wasn't what Bern had told everyone. "But that night . . ."

"What night?"

The night you kissed me and touched me, she thought. Her words, however, were different. "That night you and Bern had a fight and she went to the movies with Cindy. When you left the next day, Bern said it was just as well, she didn't want you moping around, whining because she'd broken up with you."

"Sounds like something she'd say." He turned off the main road, drove past the entrance to the state park and campgrounds, then slowed as he neared the restaurant's parking lot.

Gun Lake's popularity as a vacation spot hadn't waned over the years, and Sam's Joint was one of the best places to eat for miles around. If the number of cars and vans filling the spaces, several of them from out of state, were any indication, the restaurant was full. Effie waited until they were walking toward the entrance before she continued the conversation. "You're saying you broke up with Bern?"

"Basically. If I recall the conversation correctly, she wanted to get married and I didn't. She told me not to hold my breath waiting for her, and I told her I wouldn't. She stormed off and went out with Cindy that night, and I—"

He stopped walking and turned Effie to face him. "I became the mad groper that night, didn't I?"

The way he put it, she had to smile. "I guess you could say that."

"Will you accept my apology, thirteen years late?"

She'd always known the only reason he'd kissed her had been because he was upset with Bern. What surprised her was he remembered the incident. She grinned. "I suppose I will, if you grovel a little."

He chuckled and again turned her toward the restaurant, resting one hand on her shoulder. "I'll grovel later, after we've eaten."

Walking beside him, the top of her head barely reaching his armpit, she tried to imagine how they looked. She'd seen clown acts combining stilt walkers and midgets. That's what made people laugh: the unusual and the bizarre. If only she could laugh, it would make everything easier. Then she wouldn't be letting his hand on her shoulder turn her knees all weak and rubbery and her insides fuzzy.

Grow up, she told herself, and took in a bracing breath.

An array of scents filled the air, the strongest coming from the pine trees surrounding them and the campfires burning at the nearby campgrounds. The sun hovered above the tree line, only a few shadows hinting at the nearing of dusk. Stained-glass windows kept them from seeing inside the restaurant, but the moment Parker opened the door, they were assailed by the sounds of clattering dishes and raised voices.

"It will be about thirty minutes," the hostess said above the din, smiling graciously.

Effie wasn't surprised. On a Friday night in the summer, Sam's was always packed, and to expect anything less than a half-hour wait was foolish. She nodded when Parker asked her if that was okay.

The restaurant was comprised of various-sized rooms, each jammed with tables, the only open space being in the room with the dance floor. An L-shaped bar dominated the first room, its stools filled with customers. There was little room to stand anywhere, but Parker found a place near the entrance, out of the way of the waitresses who hurried past with overladen trays of salads and entrées, each dish looking more appetizing as time went by. Positioned behind Effie and leaning against the wall, Parker drew her close. When he put his hands on her shoulders and began massaging her arms, his fingers playing over her silk blouse, her breath caught in her throat.

"I love the feel of your shirt," he said, his words spoken close to her ear.

What she loved was the gentleness of his touch, and it took all of her willpower not to lean back against him. She was glad the noise level made conversation difficult. As breathless as she felt, she wouldn't have been able to talk. Instead, she pretended to concentrate on the restaurant's decor. Model airplanes and boats hung from the ceiling, along with Christmas lights and a full-sized canoe. A boar's head was mounted on one wall, and each room was filled with sporting equipment and musical instruments.

"Morgan, party of two!" the hostess finally called, and led them to a table in the small room near the dance floor.

Once seated, Effie searched for something to say.

Talking about Bernadette seemed safest. "I wonder if you realize the tremendous influence you had on Bern," she began. "It was after she met you that she made up her mind to go into retail."

"After she met my parents, you mean," he said. "They're the ones who were always talking to her about the retail business."

"She knew you would one day take over your father's store. She wanted to understand what interested you."

"When I saw her in Chicago, she said you're in retail."

Effie shrugged. "Co-owning a store that sells party goods hardly equals what you or Bern do. That's no little boutique she manages."

"I know. She took me through the place. I was impressed."

"The best thing about Bern is she has a level head. She doesn't let things frazzle her. She—"

Their waitress came up and asked if they wanted drinks. Effie hesitated until Parker ordered a beer, then decided that sounded good and ordered one too. As soon as the woman walked away, Effie continued. "Bern has class. Your mother said so herself."

"Yes." Parker grinned. "Mother often mentioned that to me."

Effie wondered what his mother had said about her. She decided not to ask. "Bern's also a great cook."

"What is this, anyway. A sell job? Is Bern that desperate for a husband?"

"No—no, not at all." Effie didn't want him thinking that. "Bern's not desperate at all. In fact, she's had several men propose."

"But she's never married."

It was a statement, not a question, and suddenly it

made sense to Effie. "And neither have you. Ever wonder if the reason is because you've regretted not marrying her?"

"No."

The waitress returned with their beers and took their dinner orders. Effie barely waited until the woman left before she leaned toward Parker. "Think about it. You weren't ready for marriage when you were twenty, you two broke up, but neither of you has married."

"And?"

She wasn't sure what the "and" was. She only knew it made sense. "You two always looked so good together."

Parker grinned. "I think you need a little more than 'looking good together' to make a marriage work."

"Sure, but don't tell me there wasn't more between you two." Effie remembered how they'd been, Parker always watching Bern, sneaking kisses and touching her. "I wasn't quite as naive a teenager as you thought, and I know you had Grandma and Grandpa worried when you two went off on your own."

"You're talking back when I was a teenager, when the hormones were raging."

Effie cocked her head. "You're saying when you saw Bernadette in Chicago, there were no sparks."

"Not a one."

She looked at him suspiciously, and Parker was amazed by how easily Effie conveyed her thoughts and emotions through facial expressions. He wasn't sure she even knew how expressive her look was.

"All right." He held his hand up, his thumb and index finger close together. "A little spark." Enough to inspire him to kiss Bern, but not enough to make him accept her invitation to stay for a nightcap.

Effie laughed at his answer, and he had a feeling he'd

given her a gift. Shaking his head, he gave in. "You're determined to be the matchmaker, aren't you? What do you and Cindy have up your sleeves?"

"Nothing." Effie gave him an angelic look, then grinned. "I talked Cindy into calling tonight. She's an innocent."

"I'm supposed to be relaxing while I'm here at the lake."

"Being with someone you love can be relaxing."

"With all those sparks?"

"Of course."

He disagreed. He didn't feel relaxed at the moment, but he definitely felt the sparks. They were bouncing off Effie like a sparkler on the Fourth of July, arousing his skin every time he touched her.

Their salads arrived, and he changed the subject. The person he wanted to talk about was Effie. When he'd seen Bernadette in Chicago, she'd caught him up on what Effie had been doing in the past few years, since the last time he'd seen Bern. He knew Effie had graduated from high school, had gone to Western Michigan University, and majored in art, and after graduation, had worked for an advertising agency. "About six years ago," Bern had said, "she went and did what she'd always said she would do. She became a clown. She and another woman have opened a party store in Kalamazoo." Which, according to Bern, was making them a living but little more.

He knew the facts. Now he wanted the details. "So tell me, what's it like to be a clown?"

Effie's fork stilled, a cherry tomato only inches from her mouth. Her gaze was on his face, but he doubted she saw him. From the hazy look in her eyes, her thoughts were elsewhere.

For a moment she remained in that state of suspended animation, then she looked down at her plate, her long lashes veiling her eyes. "When you bring others happiness," she said, almost on a sigh, "it's wonderful."

He expected her to go on and waited. Instead, she placed her fork and the tomato back on her plate. He saw her inhale a deep breath and hold it, and realized he'd touched on something bothering her, and now was the wrong time to push it.

He picked up the conversation with a comment on the number of new houses that had been built around the lake, and within minutes the smile was back on her face, her dimples dancing in her cheeks, and her voice filled with enthusiasm.

The barbecued ribs they'd ordered arrived about the same time the musicians playing that weekend began setting up, and by the time Effie wiped the last of the sauce from her hands and mouth, the guitar player was strumming the chords for the first song. Parker was wondering if he should ask Effie to dance when he heard another male voice calling her name.

"Effie Sanders. Just the person I wanted to see."

She looked up and smiled, and Parker turned to see a short, stocky man in his late twenties, wearing blue jeans, a western shirt, and boots, approaching the table. Parker didn't recognize him, but Effie did. "Gordon, how are you?" she asked warmly.

"Doin' great," Gordon answered, stopping beside their table. Gordon's grin took up most of his face, and Parker instantly felt jealous.

"Gordon, do you know Parker—Parker Morgan?"

"I've seen you," Gordon said, still grinning. "On television. You're the Morgan from the department store in Grand Rapids, aren't you?"

"That's me." Parker stood and shook the man's hand.

Gordon's attention switched back to Effie. "Hey, did you know that Cindy Nelson's back livin' with her folks? Her daughter's not doin' real well. Needs another operation, Cindy said."

"Parker and I ran into Cindy just this afternoon."

"She tell you how much money she needs?"

"No."

"Didn't think so. She wouldn't. Boggled my mind when I heard. The insurance she has at work pays part, but not all, so a bunch of us have decided to help out a little. We're putting on a party to raise money. Nothing big, but we're gonna have some musicians and singers, invite everyone from around here, charge admission, and give the money to Cindy."

Gordon motioned toward another table where a woman in her early twenties sat. "When I saw you over here, I told Julie, being that Cindy was such a close friend of your sister's, you'd certainly want to participate. I remember seeing you do your clown act at a show a couple years ago. You and that dog of yours were real cute. You'd be a big hit at this party."

Parker had watched Effie's expression throughout Gordon's spiel. Her smile had disappeared as she realized what he was asking, replaced by an expression of distress, even pain. Gordon finally paused, grinning in expectation of her agreement. Effie shook her head. "I can't."

Persisting, Gordon went on. "It's not like we're holding this party tomorrow. It's not until the end of the month, and even if you're not staying up here, you can drive back, can't you? What's it take you to drive up here from Kalamazoo? Forty, fifty minutes? It is for a good cause."

Again, Effie shook her head, avoiding eye contact with Gordon. "I just can't," she repeated.

Dropping his sales pitch, Gordon frowned. "Why not? We're talking a few hours of your time to help a friend of your sister's. Hell, you don't even know what date we're holdin' it, and you're sayin' no."

Parker decided Gordon's badgering had gone far enough. Gordon might not be aware of Effie's tension, but he was. "If she said she can't, she can't."

Gordon looked at him, still frowning. "All I'm asking is why not?"

"That's her business. You know Effie. If she could, she would. Just as, if I had any talent, I'd volunteer my services. I assume, however, that you're open to donations of money."

"Yeah . . ." Gordon studied Effie, then shrugged and again looked at Parker. He grinned like a jack-o'-lantern. "Always open to donations. Cindy don't know it, but we've started an account for her at the National Bank. Just make out your check to the Amanda Nelson Fund."

"I'll put one in the mail tomorrow," Parker promised, and turned to Effie. "You about ready to go?"

She nodded, her expression still tense, and Parker signaled for their waitress. Gordon said his good-byes, giving Effie one more questioning look before walking back to his table.

Parker didn't mention Gordon or the conversation on the drive back to the cottages, and Effie was uncommonly quiet, looking out the side window most of the time. Not until he pulled into his drive did she face him. "Thank you for dinner," she said, a quick smile wiping away the sadness. "I think I worked that out pretty well. I invite you to dinner, and you take me out. You sure you won't let me pay? I really should."

"Nope." The car parked, he released his seat belt and turned toward her. "This way you still owe me a home-cooked meal."

She released her own seat belt and reached for the door handle. "As soon as Bern arrives—"

He stopped her escape, catching her arm. "Afraid to be alone with me?"

"No, of course not." As if to prove her point, she let go of the door handle and faced him again. "Why would I be afraid of you?"

"I don't know, but you sure seem to want Bern around all the time."

"Only because you and Bern used to be pretty darn close . . . if I remember right."

"Well, if I remember right, you used to have a crush on me."

Her eyebrows lifted, her cheeks taking on a blush of pink, and he guessed she had thought he hadn't known. "That was thirteen years ago," she said. "I was only sixteen."

Sixteen, innocent as a lamb, and oh so tempting.

He'd given in to the temptation the night they'd sat on the dock, Bernadette off with Cindy.

What a day that had been, first Bern pushing him to get married, then his parents pushing him into a corner. They'd told him he either major in business or pay for his last two years of college on his own. It didn't matter what he wanted to do. His destiny was to run the family business. The hell with what he wanted.

Oh, he'd been in a great mood that night when he stepped outside and saw Effie sitting on the end of the dock. Somehow, he'd known she would understand. He could talk to Effie, so he did talk.

Sitting on the dock with her, he'd vented his frustration, and she'd listened. How she'd turned his anger to laughter, he'd never know. No more than he'd ever understood what happened afterward.

He'd only meant to thank her with a kiss.

How quickly he'd lost control.

He did owe her an apology. "I am sorry for the way I acted that night on the dock."

Her cheeks turned a deeper pink, and she looked at her knees, but the smile didn't disappear. "Ready to grovel now?"

"I really should. There you were, all innocent and trusting, willing to listen to my problems, and what do I do? I turn into a sex fiend."

She shrugged and looked up at him. "No big deal. You were tame compared to some of the 'fiends' I've met since."

The idea of Effie being touched by other men, sleeping with other men, bothered him. He knew it shouldn't, that he shouldn't even think of sleeping with her himself, yet he couldn't stop the feelings.

"Still friends?" she asked, extending her hand.

He took it, her fingers so small next to his. Gently, he rubbed his thumb over her knuckles and smiled. "Still friends."

She started to pull her hand free, but he tightened his hold. Friends helped friends, and he had a feeling she needed help. "Why don't you want to talk about being a clown, Effie?"

She shook her head, again trying to pull her hand away. "Just because."

"I think it's something you need to talk about."

"Well, you're wrong." She kept shaking her head and trying to free her hand. "What I need to do is go inside. It's getting late, and I still have work to do."

"You can do that after we've talked."

"What is it with you?"

Parker didn't loosen his hold. When she finally realized it was hopeless, that he wasn't going to let her go, she glared at him, then turned her head so she was staring at the garage door in front of the car. For a moment he thought she wasn't going to say a word, then she looked back.

"Okay. You want to know why I can't talk about being a clown? I'll tell you why. Have you ever been let down?" She didn't wait for an answer. "I've been let down so many times, I've lost track. I guess you could say the first time was when my mother died. After that, my father was always letting me down, making promises and then breaking them. Same with my sister, my girlfriends, and my boyfriends. People have let me down so many times in my life, I vowed never to make a promise I couldn't or wouldn't keep. But I did . . . and now I can't clown anymore."

"I don't understand."

Her look said she didn't want to go into any more detail. Finally, she did, though. "Five months ago, my grandmother had another stroke, and we had to put her in the hospital for almost a week. When they released her, she was still weak and was sent to a nursing home. I planned on moving her back into my apartment with me, but Grandma kept saying she would never leave the nursing home alive. Every day, I heard how she was going to die. I got so I didn't listen to her, simply ignored her words and assured her that she'd be coming home soon."

Effie paused for a breath, and Parker waited. When she went on, sadness filled her voice. "I guess I need to explain some other things first. You know how I always wanted to be a clown, how I loved everything and anything to do with clowns?" He nodded. "Well, a year after I graduated from college, I heard about a clown camp, where you could learn all about becoming a clown. I decided to sign up, scheduled my vacation around it, and went. For two weeks I learned about makeup, costumes, clown etiquette, and gags. I loved it.

"There was another woman there. Joan Winters. She's a couple years older than I am. We got along great from the first day and talked about how much fun it would be if we could make a living being clowns. One year later, we opened Clowning Around. Besides the party goods we sell, we entertain at parties and benefits.

"My apartment's not far from the shop, so when Grandma was living with me, I'd hop over and check on her off and on during the day. When she went into the nursing home, I always stopped by after I got off work. Except one night I was running late. Effie the Effervescent and Mopsy had been hired to do a fund-raising benefit for the Humane Society, and I wasn't going to have time to stop by and see Grandma. So I called her.

"As usual, she said she was going to die. She insisted she wouldn't make it through the night. She wanted me to stop by after the benefit so she could see me, one last time, in my clown outfit.

"She didn't sound bad, and I told her she wasn't going to die, but I did promise to stop by. I promised her." Effie looked down, shaking her head. Parker had to listen carefully when she continued.

"By the time I left the benefit, it was ten o'clock. I was sure she'd be asleep, so I went straight home and to bed. The next morning, the nursing home called and—"

Tears streamed down Effie's cheeks, and he knew the rest. Releasing her hand, he slid an arm around her shoulders, drawing her as close as he could with a console between them. "You can't blame yourself."

"Can't I?" she asked, shuddering in his embrace. "When I went over to the nursing home, the nurse who was on duty the night before told me my grandmother had waited for me to come by until midnight. 'She's going to do her clown act for me,' Grandma told her. 'Before I go.' She—"

Effie didn't finish; she didn't need to. Her next statement said it all. "I haven't been able to put on my clown outfit or makeup since."

Parker tightened his arm around her. "Or talk about it."

"Or talk about it." She looked at him. "Parker, you knew her. She was a wonderful woman. So loving and giving. She was the one person who never let me down. How could I have done that to her?"

He wished he had an answer that would ease her pain. "You didn't know."

"I should have gone. I'd promised her I would."

Touching her chin, he turned her face toward him. Her eyes were deep pools of green, her cheeks damp with tears. He didn't think about what he was doing when he kissed her lips; he simply wanted her to know that he did understand. Understood the sorrow and the guilt. To lose someone you loved was tragic; to feel you'd failed that person was devastating.

The moment his mouth covered hers, Effie tensed. He didn't push or demand, simply held her close and waited for her response. She pulled back slightly, and he let her, then he felt her relax. Wrapping her arms around his neck, she returned his kiss.

The stages from compassion to passion whirled by in a blur. Playing his lips over hers, Parker tasted the salty tears that had slid down her cheeks, and with the tip of his tongue wiped them away. She parted her lips slightly, inviting him in, and a new, shared need came into focus.

From early that morning, he'd been aroused by her. Each passing hour had brought them closer, past and present blending to create a new relationship. Desires once forbidden by age and circumstances could now be explored, and he welcomed the hunger she aroused in him.

With his hands, he soothed and caressed, stroking her shoulders and back, his fingers sliding over the smooth silk of her blouse. With his tongue, he probed and pillaged, each kiss becoming more heated; each breath, when he did breathe, becoming shakier.

The cramped interior of his car was all wrong—too confining. He wanted her closer, to feel her body pressed against his. No, he wanted her naked, lying beneath him, their bodies entwined.

"No," she groaned, as if reading his mind. She pulled back, her eyes clouded with passion and wide with surprise.

He tried to calm his harsh breathing and regain control. Thirteen years had passed, yet his reaction was the same as it had been that night on the dock, one kiss leading to another, taking him further than he'd meant to go. As on that night, so long ago, he didn't know what to say. That night he'd left her, mumbling excuses and hurrying away.

Effie was the one mumbling now, shaking her head, her hand again on the door handle.

He didn't stop her.

She left his car and walked hurriedly to her cottage, never looking back. Only when she opened her back door, letting loose a yapping, bouncing Mopsy, did her shoulders relax. He watched every movement she made, the way she scooped up the dog and carried it inside, closing the door behind her. He was still sitting behind the wheel, staring at her cottage, when she again opened the door, letting the dog out. Only then, as she waited for Mopsy to relieve herself, did Effie look toward his car.

FOUR

Effie sighed, the moist warmth of Parker's kiss light upon her cheek. In a state of euphoria, she drifted on a dream, all reality suspended. He was holding her, kissing her. Whining in her ear.

Whining?

From somewhere deep in her subconscious, Effie knew the sound wasn't right. Images flashed through her mind—feelings—and she struggled to make sense of them. There was Parker, standing by the back door of his parents' cottage, so tan and handsome. A twenty-year-old on the brink of manhood. But no, the boy was a man, touches of gray in his hair, the body not as firm and the lines on his face more deeply etched. He was coming toward her, smiling. She tried to step toward him, but movement was impossible, her feet weighted to the ground.

Again, he whined.

Or was it Bernadette whining? Effie could see her sister walking toward Parker, her blond hair flowing to her shoulders and her smile demurely proper.

"She has class," Parker's mother said, floating past.

Effie struggled to shake off the images. Far away, her grandmother was crying. Whining. "No," Effie groaned, straining to reach her grandmother. She had to get to her, had to tell her how sorry she was—

A wet tongue against her cheek brought Effie's eyes open. In the dim light of dawn, she stared at Mopsy's gray muzzle and dark button eyes. Immediately the dog barked, her tail wagging with delight. Scurrying to the edge of the bed, Mopsy jumped off, and Effie fought to come out of her stupor.

Another bark, whiny and impatient, clarified the situation, and Effie freed herself from the sheet wrapped around her legs. When Mopsy had to go, she had to go.

Still half-asleep, Effie stood in the back doorway, watching the dog make her way across the grass in search of just the right spot. The early-morning sun was turning the sky blue, and all was tranquil, the water lapping against the dock and up onto the sandy shoreline. Birds sang, the wind whispered through the treetops, and a fine mist hung above the lake like an ethereal veil.

A perfect morning.

So why did she feel so edgy?

Looking next door, Effie knew why. Sometime today she would see Parker again, and last night would loom between them. Too much had been said, too many feelings exposed. They could have forgotten the kisses they'd shared thirteen years ago, could have passed them off as a youthful mistake, but last night had changed their relationship. Never again would they simply be friends. Never again would Effie trust herself.

There were no signs of activity in his cottage. Not that she expected him to be up. The sun was barely up.

She glanced over to where Mopsy was squatting. Stifling a yawn, she flexed her shoulders. The only other people out and about, as far as she could tell, were the fishermen on the lake, their boats gently bobbing on the water as they waited for their fishing lines to produce a morning catch. Anyone with any sense—and a dog with a decent-sized bladder—was still in bed.

Her duties completed, Mopsy started back toward Effie, and Effie pushed open the screen door. Halfway to the cottage, though, the dog stopped, tracked right, and began sniffing around the base of a willow tree. "Oh, come on," Effie grumbled, then shut the door again. "All right, if you want to stay out, stay out. I'm going back to bed."

Still grumbling, she headed for her bedroom. She only got as far as the living room. The photographs and albums were still on the floor, her sorting no further along than when she'd started yesterday. In the dining room, empty cardboard boxes were stacked, waiting to be filled. A lot needed to be done in the coming days if she and Bern were going to be ready for a yard sale next Friday. This was not the time to go back to bed. A little exercise to get the body working, a quick breakfast, and she might actually get something accomplished before Bern arrived.

Quickly, she pulled on her denim shorts and a clean T-shirt, then ran her fingers through her curls. Three minutes later she was outside, the dew-damp grass wet and cool against her bare feet. Purposefully, she didn't look at the cottage next door. Facing the lake, she positioned herself on a relatively flat section of lawn, took in a deep breath, and began.

Effie was halfway through her workout when she became aware of Parker. She felt his gaze even before she caught sight of him. A half turn, and she saw him standing at his kitchen window, staring at her. Her next step was off balance, the sequence forgotten. Stumbling, she faced the lake again, made another mistake, and stopped.

She closed her eyes and breathed deeply, trying to calm the rapid beat of her heart. It didn't help. Tai chi was supposed to bring inner tranquillity.

What she was experiencing was emotional chaos.

Parker watched Effie walk back to her grandmother's cottage. Not until she reached the door did she glance his way, but even then, she kept her gaze away from his kitchen window. He heard her whistle and saw the mop of multishaded hair trot over from his dock. Tail wagging, the dog followed Effie into the cottage.

Behind Parker, his coffeepot gurgled to completion, and he shook his head. Here he was, about to drink some caffeine when his heart was already racing. What he really needed was a swift kick in the butt.

Insanity was the only excuse he could think of for his actions last night. He certainly hadn't planned that kiss. No way. It had just happened. She'd been crying, he'd been touched by her story, and he'd wanted to ease her pain.

It had nothing to do with sex.

Sure, he thought, laughing at his self-denial. And the guy in your store at Christmastime is really Santa Claus.

He could make all the excuses he wanted, but his body had a mind of its own. From the moment he'd first seen Effie yesterday, he hadn't reacted to her as a friend. And today was no different. Simply watching her move created an ache and a desire deep within him.

"Forget it!" he said aloud, and poured himself a mug of coffee.

He was at the lake to relax, and relax he would. He

was not going to let one little shrimp of a redhead get him all hot and bothered. He had other things to consider. Important things. Like what was he going to do with the rest of his life?

In her grandmother's kitchen, Effie opened a can of dog food, then paused. What had happened in Parker's car was suddenly obvious. "He felt sorry for me," she told Mopsy. "That's why he kissed me. There I was, feeling sorry for myself and . . ."

The dog danced about at her feet, whining, and Effie sighed. "You know why he kissed me?" She scooped the contents of the can into Mopsy's dish. "He felt sorry for me, that's why. Cry like a baby, and a guy will kiss you."

As Mopsy ate, Effie analyzed the events of the night before. Clowns took reality and turned it into comedy. It was time for her to take comedy and turn it into reality. "When I kissed him back he, being male, took it a step further. That's all that happened."

Leaning against the counter, she closed her eyes. If Bernadette had been around yesterday, as she should have been, Parker would have had dinner with her, and last night never would have happened. There wouldn't have been that moment of excitement when his lips touched hers, wouldn't be the longing gnawing at her insides this morning.

"Don't think of it!" she ordered herself, and opened her eyes to the stark reality of the kitchen. "It shouldn't have happened, and it won't happen again."

Mopsy gave a wag of her tail in response, but didn't leave her food. Effie didn't care. The nice thing about talking to a dog was it didn't interrupt. "I mean, so I got a little excited last night. That's no big deal. Seeing Brad

Pitt excites me, but nothing's going to come of that. I just happen to like good-looking men."

The clank of a garbage-can lid stopped her one-sided conversation. Looking out the window that faced the Morgan cottage, Effie saw Parker walking from his garbage can toward his back door. He was smiling, and just before he opened the door, he glanced her way.

Effie quickly stepped back from the window. Embarrassment twisted with chagrin, forming a knot in her stomach. Here she'd been blabbering out loud, baring her soul, and with most of the windows open.

How much had he heard?

Parker was still smiling when he placed a new bag in the wastebasket. So, Effie Sanders had gotten excited last night and considered him good-looking. It was nice to know he still had some appeal.

"You're no Brad Pitt," he acknowledged. "Still . . ."

"Dirty old man" probably best described him, but at least he wasn't walking around afraid his next breath might be his last. Not that he was sure he was healthy. What was the old saying? Don't wear your heart on your sleeve. Actually, it would be handy if people did. Then you could check it every so often.

All he knew was what the doctors had told him. Readouts of his EKG, PET, stress tests, and angiogram had shown his heart to be in good working order. It was his cholesterol levels and weight that had worried them. That and his lifestyle.

But how did you change a life planned for you from birth? He'd tried once and had failed. His mother had said it was his destiny. Like royalty, he'd inherited a title, a role in life. He was the owner and CEO of Morgan's Department Stores.

His destiny held him captive.

Effie stacked the contents of her grandmother's buffet on the carpet by the wall. Tablecloths and matching napkins were in one pile, candleholders and place mats nearby. The cottage was one of the oldest on the peninsula known as England Point. Over the years, bigger and more elaborate and expensive houses—which were still called cottages—had been built on either side. Those spacious cottages were often lived in only during the summer months. The two bedrooms, small living room, dining room, kitchen, and bathroom that made up her grandparents' cottage had been home year-round for Effie from the time she was five until she left for college. Every closet and drawer held memories.

She was emptying the last drawer in the buffet when a light knock on the screen door brought Mopsy to her feet. Barking wildly, the dog raced out of the dining room, and Effie followed. On the opposite side of the screen stood Parker, wearing khaki shorts, a green polo shirt, and sneakers.

She'd been expecting him. Waiting for him had been agony, the knot in her stomach growing larger with every passing minute. Not that she would let him know she was embarrassed or nervous. She might not be able to clown, but she could still act. Her smile was buoyant. "Good morning."

"Morning." He looked down at Mopsy, the dog's barking incessant. "She makes a good watchdog."

"Oh yeah, great." Effie pushed open the screen door, knowing exactly how Mopsy would react. Immediately, her dog turned into a wiggling bundle of happiness, sniffing at Parker's shoes and licking his ankles. "As you can see, her bark is definitely worse than her bite."

"Come on, you ferocious creature." Parker scooped up the little dog and, without hesitation, carried her into the cottage. "Saw you doing that tai stuff this morning." He paused in front of her. "You didn't finish."

"I, ah—I thought I heard the phone."

"Ah." Mopsy licked at his chin, and he put the dog back down on the floor. As he straightened, Parker's gaze traveled up Effie's body, his smile suggesting he didn't believe her. "Did you really?"

Effie knew there was no sense in lying. "No, I didn't."

"No word from Bernadette, then?"

"None."

"Any idea when she'll arrive?"

She had a guess. "Probably around noon."

"Good. That gives us time."

"Time?" Effie wasn't sure why she glanced toward her bedroom, wasn't sure why thoughts of Parker making love with her raced through her mind. She did know the knot in her stomach made another twist.

"Time for me to learn some of that tai chi stuff." He grinned and flexed his arms and shoulders, his muscles rippling. "Just something to get me started. See if I like it."

"I, ah—" Effie groped for a reason to say no. Teaching Parker self-defense was not a good move. For her own self-defense, she needed to avoid him. Grabbing the most convenient excuse, she nodded toward the dining room. "I really don't have the time now. As you can see, there's a lot to be done."

"No problem. We'll call it a trade. You help me, and I'll help you." Again, he grinned. "I'm sure there are some things on the top shelves that a 'man of height' could get for you."

His height would be helpful, but standing on a chair would be safer.

"Twenty minutes," he added before she could come up with another argument. "That's all I'm asking. A sample. You're the one who said it would be good for me."

That had been yesterday, before she'd realized how potent her attraction to him was. What was good for him might not be good for her. "There's not enough room in here."

"So? Can't we do it outside?"

Outside would be safer. People were up now, mothers watching their children in the yards, teenagers out on ski jets and water-skiing. Outside there would be space. She'd show him a couple moves, then send him on his way.

"Twenty minutes, that's all I can spare," she lied, and led the way, Mopsy trotting out with them. Near the water's edge, in clear view of everyone on the lake, she stopped and faced him. "The first thing you need to do is learn how to breathe."

He smiled, a twinkle in his eyes. "Breathing sounds like a good idea."

Effie had to agree, but at the moment she was having trouble breathing, trouble thinking straight. Her lips still burned with the memory of his kisses. Every time she looked at him, her gaze drifted to his mouth. She forced herself to focus on his stomach. "Breathe from your abdomen. Put your hand on your belly button and take in a deep breath."

Automatically, she did it herself, needing more oxygen. Parker watched, then placed his palm on his stomach, breathed in deeply, and exhaled. As she'd expected, he wasn't fully utilizing his diaphragm. He was holding in his stomach, breathing only from his chest.

"No. Extend your abdomen. Take the air down here." She pointed to a spot three fingers' width below her naval. "Center yourself."

"Show me."

Her palm on her stomach, exactly where she'd pointed, she extended her abdomen as she inhaled. Parker frowned and reached forward, touching her stomach next to her fingers. "Do it again."

She tried, but her breathing was suddenly unsteady, her focus on the touch of his fingers and the trembling in her body. Looking up, she stared into his eyes. Blue was supposed to be cool, soothing, but in his blue eyes she saw heat. Excitement.

"About last night," he said, his voice husky. "You're wrong. I wasn't just feeling sorry for you."

He had heard her that morning. She'd known he had. She had to stop talking out loud, stop spilling her guts to her dog and the whole world. "You don't have to apologize," she said.

"I wasn't going to." His satisfied smile showed no remorse. "Why apologize for something we both enjoyed?"

Enjoyed? Yes. But that didn't make it right. "It shouldn't have happened," she argued. "Once Bernadette gets here—"

"What? All will change?" The lift of his eyebrows indicated his doubt.

"Ten to one, once you see her, you'll forget I exist."

"I've never forgotten you existed."

"Oh yeah. You're saying for the last thirteen years you've been thinking about me?"

"Maybe."

"Sure." She lifted her chin in defiant denial. "That's why you didn't call, didn't write. Never came back."

"There were reasons I didn't."

"I'd love to hear them."

"You were too young at the time. I was too confused."

She shook her head. "Time doesn't stand still. I did get older."

"And my father died, leaving me in charge of the stores."

"Exactly." She understood. "Parker, you and I are total opposites."

"Haven't you heard? Opposites attract."

"They can also irritate each other. Trust me on this. Bern and I are total opposites, and I irritate the heck out of her." Effie held up one hand, lifting her index finger. "First of all, I am totally unorganized." She lifted another finger. "Second, I'm always late." Another finger went up. "Third, I'm way too emotional, I don't know when to be serious, and I don't have any class."

"I think that's three, four, and five." He placed his hand over hers, encompassing all five fingers. "You underestimate your appeal, Ms. Sanders. Last night, I didn't kiss you just because you were crying. I kissed you because you are one sexy lady."

"I also talk too much. And to a dog, no less." She glanced down at the large masculine hand covering hers, then looked back up. "Parker, this is crazy."

"I agree. The timing is rotten, and all your arguments are probably valid." He squeezed her fingers. "But I'm glad you talked to me last night. I've thought about what you said. I know you feel guilty about not going to see your grandmother, but you shouldn't. Maybe what you need to do is dedicate every performance you do as a clown to her."

Effie shook her head and drew her hand away from his. "You sound like Kent, my last boyfriend. He had all the answers, the quick fix. He told me it was all in my mind, that I was being ridiculous." She could still hear his words. " 'Deal with it,' he said. Only it wasn't that easy." She looked down at the grass by their feet. "I can't deal with it."

Gently, Parker touched her under her chin, forcing her to look up at him. "I understand. In fact, I know exactly what you're feeling. We're not as opposite as you might think."

Effie bit her lower lip, and he could see the tears pooling in her eyes, turning them a liquidy green. Her pain was raw and cut through him, and he drew her close, wishing he could hug away her guilt. Wishing he could hug away his own guilt.

That she allowed him to hold her surprised him, and he savored the warmth of her body against his, all the while trying not to react physically. Neither of them was ready for a relationship. Maybe that's why he was drawn to her, because she needed him, just as he needed her. One friend helping another.

How to convince his body that Effie was only a friend was the problem. He was growing hard simply holding her. "So how do I breathe?" he asked, not certain he could breathe the way his heart was pounding. A month ago, if he'd felt this way, he would have been in a panic. Today, he understood his reaction.

Without pulling away, Effie slid a hand between them, her fingertips resting just below the waistband of his shorts. Instantly, his efforts to control his physical reactions failed, and he hoped she didn't move her fingers any lower or she was going to know exactly why he wasn't breathing.

"Take in a deep breath," she ordered. "So you push my fingers out."

Something else might be pushing her fingers out in a minute, he thought. Gritting his teeth, he sucked air in, expanding his waistline.

"Good. Now pull your stomach in as you let that air out."

He did, waiting for her hand to drop, half hoping it would and half praying it wouldn't.

She stepped back, out of his embrace. The smile was back in her eyes, her cheeks dimpled. "Perfect."

"I'm a quick learner."

"Good." Effie positioned herself by his side. "Then I'll show you commencement."

She spaced her feet a shoulder's width apart, dropped her arms to her sides, and took in a deep breath, expanding her abdomen. Her expression was serious, and he caught the quick glance she gave him as she let out her breath. An auburn eyebrow lifted in question, and he obliged by mimicking her position.

She repeated the movement. "Think of being in water that comes to your shoulders. Let your hands rise to the surface, straight out in front of you, palms down, and as you do, take in a breath."

She did as she'd instructed, and he copied, more interested in watching her than in what he was learning. The clown was gone, replaced by the teacher. He was the one who felt silly. "I think you just drowned," he said, his hands a good foot above hers. "Water's over your head."

She ignored him. "Now bring your hands to your shoulders, palms facing out. Then press them down to your sides as you exhale."

Again, she did as she'd instructed, and he heard the

sweet sigh of her released breath. He played the copy-cat, ending up with his hands by his sides.

"That's commencement," she said, stepping away. "And this is cessation."

Waving her right hand, she stepped back toward her grandmother's cottage. By her fourth step, Parker realized what she was doing. "I take it that's the end of the lesson."

"Work calls," she said, stopping the waving but continuing to retreat to the cottage.

He walked after her. "So what are we doing?"

"We?" She stopped.

"I promised I'd help."

"Don't you have a golf game or something?"

He shrugged. He had planned on getting in nine holes before it got too hot, but it wasn't anything set in stone.

"Go play golf," she said.

"One kiss and you're already turning into a nag."

She blushed, and he knew she hadn't expected him to mention that kiss, not that offhandedly. "It's for your own good," she said, some of the lightness gone from her voice.

"Maybe being around you is for my own good."

She took another step toward her door. "Come back later."

"How much later?"

"This afternoon."

When Bern was there. He wasn't that slow to catch on. The matchmaker was at work again. Well, maybe it would be better if he stopped by that afternoon. Effie could be right. Seeing Bern again might change his feelings. There was only one way to find out. "It's a deal. Say, two o'clock?"

"I'll save all the high-level assignments for you," she said with a grin, and whistled for Mopsy.

Parker waited until she was almost inside the cottage, then he threw one more comment her way. "You liked that kiss, and you're a liar if you deny it."

FIVE

Mopsy announced Bernadette's arrival, and as Effie had guessed, it was nearly noon. Effie also wasn't surprised that Bern looked as though she'd just stepped from the cover of a fashion magazine. That her sister's hair was snugged into a twist without a strand out of place, her makeup was flawless, and her shorts outfit was fashionable and expensive merely supported how different they were. People meeting them for the first time found it difficult to believe they were sisters. Only those who had known their mother understood.

Bernadette Sanders was the image of Carolyn Daves Sanders, while Effie favored her father's side of the family, especially her grandmother. The pictures she'd been going through since arriving at the lake confirmed that. Over the years, the red had faded from her grandmother's hair, but it had once been there. She'd had curls and green eyes too. Effie wasn't sorry she looked like her grandmother, but there were times she wished she'd inherited her mother's height and darker complexion.

Bernadette swooped into the cottage and scooped up

Mopsy, cooing over the dog like an aunt with a favored niece. Mopsy lapped up every moment, her tail wagging and her body wiggling.

"And how are you, my little cutie?" Bern asked, putting her face close to the dog's.

Effie grinned when Mopsy licked Bernadette's nose. Bern's grimace ended the conversation, and Mopsy was put back on the floor. The dog danced about on her hind legs, begging for more attention, but Bern was looking at Effie. "And how are you doing?"

The simple question was Effie's downfall. Emotions too close to the surface welled over in tears. Bern stepped forward and embraced her, surrounding her with the scent of expensive perfume. Her soft silk scarf tickled her nose, and Effie sighed.

Months had passed since she'd last seen her sister. Then they had hugged and cried, standing together to bear the death of their grandmother. For almost all of their lives they'd stood together, so different, yet sharing the same loss of a mother and an ever-absent father. Without realizing it, Effie had missed her sister. "I'm glad you're here."

"So am I." Bernadette released her and stepped away, looking around the cottage. "It's been a while. Funny, I'd forgotten how small this place is. It's not much bigger than my apartment."

"I hope you don't have as much stuff in your apartment as there is here." Effie wiped away the tears and laughed. "I swear Grandma kept everything."

"And I've put us one day behind." Bern headed for the door. "I'll get my things."

"Parker's here."

Bernadette stopped, turning to look back. "Really?"

"He had some kind of stress attack a couple months

ago, thought he was having a heart attack, and the doctor told him he had to relax."

"So he came here, to the lake?"

Effie nodded. "I had dinner with him last night."

Bernadette cocked her head, a carefully plucked eyebrow rising. "Now that sounds interesting."

"You were the one who was supposed to have dinner with him." She wanted Bern to understand what had happened wasn't something she'd planned. "Cindy and I had it all worked out."

"Cindy? Cindy Nelson? She's here at the lake?"

"She's back living with her parents." There was so much to tell Bern. "Her daughter's not doing well, needs another operation, but is depressed, and—"

Bern lifted a hand, stopping her. "Why don't you tell me everything later? Right now I want to get my bag, freshen up, and—" She glanced out the door toward Parker's place. "Is he over there now?"

"I don't think so." Effie hadn't seen him since his quicky tai chi lesson that morning. "I think he's playing golf."

"How long's he staying?"

"A couple weeks."

Bern's smile wiped away any hopes Effie had that Bern wouldn't be interested. "Two weeks," she repeated, and Effie could almost see her sister planning her strategy.

"He said he'd come over this afternoon to see if we needed any help."

"And, of course, we will." Bern nodded and pushed open the screen door. "I can't believe how perfect this is." Again she smiled at Effie. "You are a doll for suggesting we do this this week."

❖━━━❖

Parker knew Bernadette was at the cottage. He recognized her sporty white Acura parked beside Effie's Ford. He'd ridden in the car only six months earlier, the night they'd gone out. It was classy, but then, his mother had always said Bernadette had class. Both of his parents had liked her. "She's the type you should marry," his father had said more than once. "She may be young, but she has the looks and the brains you're going to want in a wife."

Parker had thought he agreed . . . until Bern began pushing to get married.

She's been waiting for you, and you've been waiting for her. Effie's words rang through his head.

Could it be true?

If so, he hadn't realized it the day he saw Bern in Chicago. That date hadn't stirred him into wanting to be with her. Not as he now wanted to be with Effie, even after leaving her only a few hours ago.

Not even nine holes of golf had eased the tension she'd created in his body. She'd shown him the moves for commencement. Well, he wanted to show her the moves for climax.

Parked in his driveway, he didn't get out of his car. He knew the way he was acting was ridiculous. He was back to his teens, experiencing a hormonal overdose. He had to stop thinking of sex.

A movement past a window in the Sanderses' cottage caught his attention. He wasn't surprised when Bernadette stepped back and looked out, directly at him. Her wave and smile were warm, but controlled. Bern had never shown the spontaneity that was part of Effie's nature.

When Bern walked away from the window, he knew she was coming outside. Sucking in a deep breath, he pulled in his stomach, then remembered Effie's commands. "Breathe deep. Center yourself."

He needed to center himself. At the moment he felt completely off center.

Effie heard the screen door bang shut. Standing, she stretched cramped muscles and glanced out the window. Bernadette walked past, toward the Morgan's cottage. A second later Effie saw Parker.

Fascinated, she watched, even while the acid of jealousy churned in her stomach and her need for self-preservation begged her to turn away. Bernadette's carefully schooled actions flowed from one to the next. A smile. An embrace and a peck on Parker's cheek. Effie could hear a few words, but Bern kept her voice low. She got the response she wanted. Parker leaned close to catch what Bernadette was saying, his body and emotions now hers to command.

He patted his stomach, sucking in the muscles, and nodded, his smile indicating his pleasure. Effie remembered the feel of those stomach muscles beneath the palm of her hand. They'd been tensed and warm.

He'd wanted her that morning. Now he was responding to Bern.

Thirteen years of maturity slipped away as old insecurities and feelings surfaced and Effie did turn from the window. Why watch? As a birthday-party clown, she'd learned that when it came time for the gifts, she would be forgotten. Bernadette was the perfect gift, her packaging stylish and promising.

Already, Parker had forgotten the clown.

Moments later Bernadette came through the door, her smile triumphant. "I'm going to take a break. I need some aspirin, and Parker said he'd drive me to the store."

Bern walked back toward the bedrooms, and Effie didn't bother telling her there was a bottle of aspirin in the kitchen. She knew the trip had nothing to do with aspirin. Bern wanted time alone with Parker.

"We won't be long," he said. The sound of his voice was surprisingly close, and Effie turned to find him standing just outside the screen door. "I'll be back to fulfill my part of the bargain."

Mopsy wagged her tail at the sight of him, but didn't bark. Effie stayed where she was. "What bargain?"

"To help you in exchange for the tai chi lesson."

She shook her head. "That was hardly a lesson."

"Merely a commencement?" His smile suggested there'd be more to follow.

She doubted it. "Could you get more boxes while you're at the store?" she asked, hoping she sounded as though she didn't care that he was going with Bern. "I thought I had enough, but there's more stuff here than I expected."

"Will do." He looked past her, and Effie knew Bern had come back into view. His smile was now for her.

"We won't be long," Bern promised, echoing Parker's words.

Effie said nothing, but when she heard Parker's car drive off, she glanced at the clock. Two-fifteen.

Bernadette returned at four, carrying three empty boxes. "This is all they had right now, but they'll have more on Monday." She glanced at the slender watch on her wrist. "Parker asked me out to dinner. I'll work for two hours, then get ready. Also, I told him we wouldn't need his help today, to come over tomorrow."

Effie glanced at the books she'd left on the top shelves of the bookcases in the living room. The disappointment cutting through her had nothing to do with those books or when they would be sorted and put into boxes. Much as she hated to admit it, she'd been looking forward to seeing Parker again, to hearing his smooth, masculine voice.

So, turn on the TV and watch one of his ads, she told herself, knowing she was beating her head against a wall. Bern was in control. Parker was now hers.

"That was quite an experience he had two months ago," Bern said, looking out the window that faced Parker's cottage.

"He didn't say much about it to me," Effie said, hurt that he hadn't.

Bern glanced at her. "It really shook him up."

"You two are getting along pretty well, I take it?"

Bernadette's smile glowed. "Let's just say I can tell he's interested in what I have to offer. I can't believe how perfect the timing is, for both of us."

"Almost like providence stepped in."

Bern shrugged. "If you believe in that sort of thing. I like to think that opportunity has knocked, and I'm going to let it in."

"Meaning?"

"Meaning the man's had a scare, thought he was going to die. Six months ago when I saw him in Chicago, all he could talk about were those stores. Now—" Bern smiled, then lifted an eyebrow. "He said you gave him a tai chi lesson this morning."

"He asked me to," Effie said, not wanting to cause any jealousy. "He saw me doing the routine yesterday morning, and I suggested he might want to try it since he'd said he needed to relax. I meant for him to take lessons, not that I would teach him."

"He said he liked what you showed him." Bern continued smiling, but Effie sensed her sister was digging.

"I didn't show him much. Just the first move."

"He also said you're cute."

Effie wasn't sure she was flattered. She wanted to be beautiful. Sexy. Sophisticated. "He's always thought I was cute . . . like a puppy."

Bern laughed and glanced at Mopsy. "He did mention your dog was cute too."

"See. There's no need to be jealous. You're the one he's always had eyes for."

"I'm not jealous, and don't sell yourself short, little sister."

Bern gave her a quick glance from head to toes, and Effie laughed. "If I sell myself, it has to be as short. Five feet is hardly considered tall."

"You know what I mean. If you'd wear more makeup, dress a little more stylishly . . ."

Shaking her head, Effie went back to marking boxes. "You know that's not me."

"You put makeup on when you dress as a clown."

"And I'm not even doing that anymore." Effie looked up at her sister. "You're the type men like Parker go for. By tonight, you'll have him eating out of your hand."

Bern grinned. "Well, in a way, I hope you're right."

Parker walked the distance between the two cottages at exactly seven o'clock. Mopsy barked when he knocked on the front screen door, came dashing out of the kitchen, and raced straight for him. The moment she recognized him, she began wagging her tail. Another yip, this one welcoming, brought Effie out of the kitchen. "Parker's here," she yelled toward the bed-rooms.

"Tell him I'll be a minute," Bern yelled back.

Parker tapped the face of his watch. "What's your guess?"

"A lot longer than a minute," Effie said, and opened the screen door to let him in. "Come on in and set a spell."

"That's what your grandfather always used to say." He still remembered the old man and his easygoing way. "What's missing is the TV being on." Parker stepped into the cottage and glanced around. The photo albums and pictures were now on the dining-room table, and stacks of boxes, each labeled with its contents, filled the living room. "You've done a lot since last night. Sorry for not coming over this afternoon. Bern said you could use me more tomorrow afternoon."

"No problem," Effie said, and shrugged. "I didn't really expect you."

"I did promise to help."

She laughed, but it didn't translate to her body. "Promises, promises."

"Are not always broken." He prided himself in keeping his promises. "I will be here tomorrow."

"Whatever you say." Turning away, she headed back toward the kitchen. "I've got to check on my pasta."

Parker watched her disappear through the doorway. She'd been polite and friendly, but the sparkle was missing. You're taking her sister out, he reminded himself, aware that it was not wise to date one woman while trying to impress another, especially when the two were sisters.

That Effie wasn't acting naturally was actually encouraging. If she had been as bubbly as usual, all smiles and laughter, he would have wondered if she cared. A few signs of jealousy were good. Nothing dramatic, just a sense that something was bothering her.

He wanted to bother her. She was certainly bothering him.

He followed her to the kitchen, leaned against the doorjamb, and watched her drain a pot of cooked shells. He said nothing, but he knew she was aware of his presence. The fact that she didn't look at him as she chilled the shells under cold water was interesting, along with the numerous times she licked her lips. The darting of her tongue led his mind in directions he wanted to avoid. He had to say something. "Bern said she wanted to talk to me about business. That's why I didn't ask you to join us."

"No problem." Effie barely gave him a glance.

"She said she had some ideas on how I could spend less time at the store."

"Good." Effie dumped the cooled shells into a glass bowl that contained cut-up vegetables.

"I'm not playing one sister off the other."

"I never thought—" She looked at him, then back down at the salad she was making. "You don't need to explain."

"I think I do." Desultory responses were not typical of Effie Sanders. "After all, I did kiss you last night."

Her head rose swiftly as she glanced at him, then toward the bedrooms. "What happened last night . . . well, it just happened," she said, her voice barely above a whisper. "I think the best thing to do is forget it."

"Can you?"

One side of her mouth twitched, relaying her struggle to deny the truth. Quickly, she looked away. "Yes."

"Well, I'm not going to . . . no more than I've forgotten the time I kissed you on the dock, thirteen—"

"Parker, shh." Frowning, Effie walked toward him. "Bern will hear."

"And?" He wanted to know what Effie was thinking.

She stopped far enough back that he couldn't reach her without moving, and she kept her voice low. "Bern likes you."

"I like her." He also dropped the level of his voice. "And I like you."

"Yes, but you don't want Bern thinking there's something going on between us when there's not."

"Isn't there?"

She stared at him, and he smiled. He wasn't sure himself what was going on between them. Reasonably, nothing should be, but then, he hadn't been acting reasonably since seeing her yesterday morning.

"It's just that—" she started, then stopped as her gaze slipped to his mouth.

The flush of color in her cheeks gave a clue to her thoughts, along with the way she licked her lips. When her gaze again met his, he knew, reasonable or not, that the chemistry was there. The desire to repeat the kiss they'd shared the night before was not one-sided.

"I—" She tried again, her voice shaky with emotion.

Another voice cut her off. "I'm ready," Bernadette announced, coming down the short hallway.

Effie hurried back to the counter, and by the time Bern had stepped up beside him, Effie's attention was on the salad she was preparing. To Bernadette, it would appear he'd been having a casual conversation with Effie, as he had so many times in the past when he'd waited for Bern to get ready and Effie had entertained him. This time, however, he knew things were different. This time, he didn't want to leave Effie. "Why don't you come with us?" he asked her.

She looked back, clearly surprised that he'd asked.

Her gaze focused on Bernadette, and Effie shook her head. "You two have a good time."

"We will," Bern said smoothly, and slipped an arm through his. "Don't wait up."

Effie had no intention of waiting up. By nine-thirty, she was ready to go to bed. She'd had a long day and hadn't slept all that well the night before. A good night's sleep was what she needed, she told herself. Then she'd be thinking clearer. Then she could handle the crazy thoughts that ran through her head every time she saw Parker.

By ten-thirty, she knew sleep wasn't going to come all that easily. Tossing and turning, she'd disturbed Mopsy, who'd finally jumped off the bed and curled up on the carpet. By eleven, Effie was ready to scream. She'd counted sheep, had planned her course of attack for the next day of packing, had mentally worked out how she would tell her partner she wasn't going to clown anymore, and had explained to herself, at least a dozen times, why she shouldn't be thinking about Parker, why she was a fool to hope what he'd said in the kitchen had meant anything.

By eleven-fifteen Effie was out of bed. She didn't want to think anymore, and she'd certainly packed enough books that afternoon to find one that would hold her interest. Not bothering with a robe or slippers, or even to turn on a light, she went into the living room, Mopsy by her feet. She was about to turn on a light there when she glanced out the window and saw Bernadette and Parker. They were seated on the end of the dock, at exactly the same spot where he'd sat with her thirteen years ago. Effie didn't want to watch, yet she couldn't look away.

Silhouetted in the moonlight, Bernadette turned toward Parker. She slipped her arms around his neck, drew his head close, and kissed him. Effie watched, unable to stop the nausea building in her stomach or the tightness around her heart. The air surrounding her grew thin, breathing impossible. All her denials turned to dust. She did care.

She did want what she couldn't have.

Squeezing her eyes shut, she turned and made her way back to her bedroom. She couldn't have read a book if she'd wanted to. The pain was too great, the desolation. She didn't want to cry, but the tears came, silently slipping down her cheeks.

Mopsy hopped back up on the bed, and Effie drew the dog close, hugging her. Mopsy licked away the tears, whining softly. Effie absorbed the sound, letting it soothe her. Then the creak of the screen door being opened brought a sharp bark of warning from Mopsy, jarring Effie's senses. Wiggling free from Effie's arms, Mopsy jumped off the bed.

Effie didn't call her back. In silence she listened.

"Shh," Bernadette whispered to the dog. "It's just me."

"I'll see you tomorrow, then," Parker said, his voice also hushed.

"I'll be waiting."

There was silence, and Effie could imagine what was happening. In her mind, she could see Parker kissing Bern, holding her close and touching her. Squeezing her eyes shut, she tried to block out the memories of his mouth on hers, his tongue slipping between her lips, and his hands, so large and warm, roaming over her back . . . under her T-shirt.

Shaking her head back and forth on the pillow, tears sliding errantly from beneath her lids, she held in the pain. Only when Mopsy jumped back on the bed, landing directly on Effie's stomach, did she groan.

"You still awake?" Bern asked from the doorway.

Effie drew in a breath and tried to keep her voice level. "Sort of."

She heard Bern's sigh of pleasure. "Things are looking up for me, kiddo. I think this is going to work."

"Hope so," was all Effie dared to say.

Again, Bern sighed, and in spite of the darkness, Effie could practically see her sister's smile. "What a difference thirteen years can make in a man. Now that I look back, we were both so young then. Now . . ." One more sigh, deep and dreamy, escaped from Bernadette, then she laughed. "Things are definitely looking up."

Effie knew she couldn't say anything, not without letting Bern know how she felt. Biting her lip, she lay in the darkness, each breath an effort.

"Well, good night," Bern said softly, and Effie heard her walk on to the next bedroom.

That Bernadette had decided to use their grandparents' bedroom while here was a blessing. Effie knew she wouldn't have been able to disguise her feelings if Bern had shared the room and bed with her. At some point, Bern would have realized something was wrong.

Effie rubbed her fingers through Mopsy's dense coat, cuddling the warm dog close to her body. Tears were a waste of time. So was jealousy. It wasn't Bern's fault that Parker had kissed her little sister last night and aroused her hopes. It probably wasn't even Parker's fault. He was confused. Scared by that stress attack he'd had.

He was a man, and Effie had learned not to trust what men said. What they wanted today might not be what they wanted tomorrow. Just like her father, men couldn't be depended on. If she wanted to find happiness, she was going to have to depend on herself, no one else.

"The best thing for you to do," she murmured to herself, "is stay as far away from Parker as you can."

SIX

Effie wasn't quite sure how she was going to avoid being around Parker when he'd promised to help. She considered the problem the next morning as she and Bern went through their grandparents' medicine cabinet. "Do you have any idea when Parker's coming over today?" she asked.

"Probably sometime this afternoon," Bern said, then opened a blue container and grinned. "Think someone would want to buy half a set of false teeth?" She showed the dentures to Effie. "We could advertise them as new. Grandma said Grandpa never would wear the lower ones."

"I thought she'd thrown those away."

"Grandma?" Bern tossed the container and teeth into the wastebasket, to join a multitude of medicines and health aids long past their expiration dates. "I'm beginning to understand why Dad has this obsession to dig up old things. It's in the Sanders blood to keep things forever."

"Not this Sanders," Effie said. "As soon as I get back

to my apartment, I'm tossing anything and everything I haven't used in the last six months."

A box of gauze, never opened, was placed among the items they would keep for the yard sale. Used razors went into the wastebasket. Inch by inch, they worked through the bathroom. Effie's thoughts, however, weren't on what to sell and what to toss but on Parker.

Seeing him kiss Bernadette the previous night had been harder to take than she'd expected. It was one thing to tell herself Bern was perfect for Parker, another to forget how his lips had felt on hers. As a clown, she'd learned to act, to keep smiling even when she was sad. She'd thought it was only the makeup and costume she couldn't put on, but Effie wasn't sure she could smile and pretend all was well around Parker.

"You wouldn't mind if I took off when he gets here, would you?" she asked, hoping the question sounded casual. "I was thinking of going around this afternoon and seeing if I could find some of the old gang."

Bern shrugged. "I don't care. I've got to get over to see Cindy myself." She ran a fingertip over the surface of the top shelf. "This is filthy. Do we have any cleaning solvent?"

"In the kitchen. I'll get it." Effie dropped a half-used bottle of hand lotion into the wastebasket and started for the kitchen. She was in the living room when Mopsy dashed by her and began barking at the screen door. Effie called to her, then she saw Parker walking toward the cottage.

His clothes were similar to the day before—a striped polo shirt, blue shorts, and sneakers—and his stroll was relaxed. He looked happy, and she knew why. Bernadette.

Picking up Mopsy, Effie silenced her barks and waited for Parker to reach the door. His smile irritated her; that he'd come before she could escape irritated her. "You're earlier than Bern expected . . . that is, if you've come to help."

"That's why I'm here." He let himself in. "Just couldn't stay away."

She put Mopsy down and nodded toward the back of the cottage. "Bern's in the bathroom."

She started for the kitchen, but Parker caught her arm, stopping her. "You didn't do your tai chi this morning."

"I got up late." A lame excuse for not wanting to chance seeing him.

"So when do I get my next lesson?"

He kept hold of her arm, his smile intoxicating and a teasing glint in his eyes. He'd always teased her, but this morning, she wasn't in the mood. If he wanted a lesson, she'd give him one. Decisively, she stepped toward him. "This is called 'ward off.' "

With a twist of her wrist, she brought her arm back toward her body, pressed forward with her opposite hand, and pushed his hand away. The move worked as it was intended, catching him off guard. In a second she was free from his grasp and stepping back.

"Very impressive," he said with an approving nod.

"Comes in handy sometimes." Again, she glanced toward the bathroom. "Now, if you'll excuse me, I need to get some cleaning solvent for Bern."

Effie headed for the kitchen, expecting Parker to join Bernadette in the bathroom. Instead, he followed her. "I imagine you've had to fight off a lot of men."

"Oh, all the time," she lied, wishing he would go away . . . and that her heart rate would drop back to normal. As many men as she had known in her twenty-nine years, none had ever flustered her as Parker could.

For a second she wasn't sure why she was in the kitchen. Then she remembered.

Her grandmother had kept her cleaning products under the sink. Effie opened the cabinet door, crouched down, and glanced over the containers. She sensed as well as heard Parker come up beside her. His bare legs were in her peripheral view. They were well-muscled legs, with a light covering of dark hairs. Sturdy legs.

Sexy legs.

Get your mind off sex, she scolded herself, angry that she couldn't ignore her attraction to him. Angry that she'd gotten herself into this mess.

"Looking for anything special?" he asked, crouching beside her.

She caught the scent of his aftershave, and kept her gaze focused on the bottles. His right knee was only inches from hers, his shoulder nearly touching hers. Psychological abuse came in many forms. This was one.

"Something to clean the shelves of the medicine cabinet," she managed to say, disturbed by how breathless her voice sounded.

"What about this?"

His arm brushed against hers as he reached for a bottle directly in front of her. A surge of heat flowed through her body, flushing her face. "That—that's fine."

She took the bottle from his hand and quickly stood, needing space between them and air to breathe. Leaning against the counter, she tried to cover her reaction. "Feels like it's going to be another scorcher of a day. Can you believe how hot it is already?"

He smiled up at her and rose slowly. "Quite hot."

"They're predicting thunderstorms this afternoon."

Parker stepped closer, his gaze never leaving her face and his smile too knowing. Effie wasn't sure what to do.

To move would tell him he was bothering her. But to stay—

Parker knew the flush in Effie's cheeks had nothing to do with the outside temperature. No more than the electricity passing between them was caused by ionic pressure. The brightness of her eyes and the way she was fidgeting said more than her words. His presence disturbed her.

Well, her presence disturbed him.

"What are you two up to?" Bernadette asked from the doorway.

A look of guilt swiftly crossed Effie's face. "We, ah—that is, I, ah—"

"We found some cleaning solvent," he said, amused by Effie's flustered response. She reminded him of a kid caught with her hand in the cookie jar.

"Good." Bernadette's smile was enigmatic as she walked regally over to the sink.

Effie held up the bottle of cleaner, but Bern didn't look. She got a glass from the cupboard and turned on the water, and Parker let his gaze play between the two women.

The dynamics were interesting. Effie's body language was open and expressive; she wasn't sure of herself or what was going on. Bernadette's behavior was controlled. Perhaps too controlled. Parker wasn't sure what she was thinking. Last night, she'd made it clear she was interested in a job. She'd also made it clear she wouldn't be opposed to reestablishing their relationship.

He shouldn't have kissed her.

"I, ah . . ." Effie stepped away from him, heading for the door. "I'll go get started on those shelves."

He watched her walk out of the kitchen, then looked back at Bernadette. Her gaze was focused on him, and he knew they had to talk. "She's changed in the last thirteen years," he said.

"Not that much. She's always had a crush on you."

"Thirteen years ago, she was a child."

"She's no child now."

"No, she's not."

Bern walked toward him, her hair loose and flowing to her shoulders, her subtle makeup enhancing her beauty. Smiling, she looked up at him through long, silvery lashes. "Time changes a lot of things."

Her eyes were the blue of the lake at its deepest point, mysterious and alluring. Memories of the past teased at his subconscious. They'd had good times together. She'd been his first love, and a man never forgot that. Memories, however, weren't enough.

Last night he'd given it a try, had honestly wondered if the sparks could be rekindled. Over dinner, they'd reminisced about the three summers they'd spent together. On the dock, he'd kissed her.

As wonderful as those three summers had been, the past was not today. Thirteen years ago, they'd been two teenagers learning and exploring the mysteries of sex. Back then, he'd thought Bernadette was the woman he wanted. Back then, he'd been confused, his wants mixed up with his parents' wants.

Would he have ended up with Bernadette if she hadn't chosen that time in his life to push to get married?

He would never know.

It seemed he had a knack for getting involved with the Sanders women at the wrong time in his life. Smiling at Bern, he shook his head. "Sometimes I wonder if time changes anything."

Effie sprayed solvent on the shelves in the medicine cabinet and scrubbed them clean with a sponge. She had to stand on the toilet lid to reach the top shelf. She could hear Bernadette and Parker in the kitchen, their voices too low to make out the words. Every so often one would laugh, Parker's chuckle a deep rumble and Bern's light and just a little stilted.

"Relax, Bern," she ordered, the command traveling no farther than the doorway of the bathroom. She knew her sister could be a lot of fun when she wasn't trying to control a situation. Bern was simply too serious for her own good.

And you? Effie asked herself.

She needed to get serious.

This getting all hot and flustered just because Parker's arm had brushed against hers was ridiculous. He was a man, nothing more. A good-looking man, yes. And a great kisser.

She shook her head and rubbed harder with the sponge. She wasn't going to think about him kissing her. It had happened, she understood why, and the best thing for her to do was forget it. Or if not forget it, at least get it into perspective.

His kisses had meant nothing, and neither did his teasing. She had to stop getting all flustered, had to stop acting like a silly teenager. She had to—

"How's it going in here?" Parker asked, poking his head into the bathroom.

Startled, Effie dropped the bottle of cleaning solvent, and it hit the sink basin with a thunk. From her perch on the toilet, she stared at the bottle, then at him. Five minutes of self-lecture, and she was still acting like a teenager. His one question had increased her pulse rate threefold, and his smile wasn't helping her aplomb.

Parker reached into the sink and retrieved the bottle.

Fortunately, the top had stayed on. Saying nothing, he held it out to her. She groped for a witty comment, but only came up with, "Thanks."

"No problem." He glanced around the room. "What's your plan of attack?"

"Plan of attack?" She laughed. "That's where you're like Bern. You two plan. I just attack."

He nodded to the medicine cabinet. "Want me to clean the top of that for you?"

"No, thanks." What she wanted was him out of the room. "You could, however, get the books on the top shelves in the living room and put them in boxes. We're sorting according to subject matter. The boxes are marked."

"Your wish is my command." He gave a slight bow and backed out of the room.

Effie closed her eyes and wished for strength.

As the morning progressed Effie also wished her grandparents' cottage was bigger. How four people had lived there year-round without constantly colliding now amazed her. No matter what room she worked in, she kept bumping into Parker. Each time, it was her fault, or so it seemed. She'd be working on a project, would remember something she wanted and go to get it, only to discover Parker, in his organized, methodical manner, was right in her pathway. After the third time it happened, she stopped making excuses. If he thought she was trying to run into him, he was wrong. She wanted him back with her sister.

He and Bernadette were meant for each other, she kept telling herself.

The words, however, didn't stop the physical reactions she experienced every time he was near. By midday, she knew she had to get away. "Mopsy and I are going for a drive," she said to Bernadette and Parker. They were sitting at the kitchen table, making lists of items to be sold. "I think I'll pick up some more cleaning supplies and—"

Parker pushed his chair back and stood, rotating his shoulders as he did. "Good. I'll go with you. It's after twelve, and I'd like some beer."

"But, I—" Effie wanted to get away from Parker, not take him with her.

"And could you pick up some iced tea for me?" Bernadette asked, wiping at her forehead with the back of her hand. "Any flavor. If it gets any muggier, I'm going to melt. Why didn't Grandpa put in air-conditioning?"

"Money," Effie said. Her escape was turning into a mission. "Anything else?"

Bern glanced at another list on the table. "Well, as long as you're going, we need these items."

Effie took the list. Included were items she'd mentioned earlier: masking tape and colored marking pens. Bern had added upholstery cleaner. Effie agreed. The chairs would bring better prices if the stains were removed. Bern had also added a few food and pharmacy items. Hoping she sounded casual, Effie said to Parker, "You don't need to come along. I can get that beer for you. What kind do you want?"

He shook his head. "I need a break, and I want to see if they have a pricing gun we could use to mark things. It would sure make it easier."

"But—"

An ominous rumble of thunder interrupted her, and Parker took her arm and turned her toward the door. "We'd better get going or we're going to be rained on."

"You don't need to come along," she insisted, even as he guided her to the door. "I can get everything."

"And I can help." He pushed open the screen. "Your car or mine?"

"Mine." She wanted some control over the situation. She certainly hadn't succeeded in escaping him.

Lightning flashed off in the distance, then more thunder shook the sky. Effie hurried to let Mopsy into her car, then herself. She wasn't sure if it was the electricity in the air, but the moment Parker slid into the seat next to her, she felt sparks.

"Weicks all right?" she asked. The grocery-pharmacy combination store was the most likely place to have everything on the list.

"Sounds fine."

As Effie pulled her car out onto the street, Mopsy wiggled between the seats and onto Parker's lap. Effie glanced his way, curious to see his reaction. He didn't push the dog back. Laughing, he positioned Mopsy so she could look out the window, and Mopsy rewarded him with a quick lick on his chin.

"At least *she's* not trying to avoid me," he said.

He saw the guilt in Effie's expression and knew he'd guessed right. All morning she'd been making excuses, giving reasons why she needed to be in another room than the one he was in. Empty excuses.

"I haven't been avoiding you," she said, but didn't look at him.

"Could have fooled me."

"How about all those times I bumped into you . . . or practically bumped into you?"

"Wouldn't have happened if you hadn't been so busy trying to avoid me." And those run-ins hadn't been entirely accidental. He'd seen to that.

"I just—" She hesitated, and he waited. "I just feel you and Bern should be spending as much time together as possible."

"Still playing the matchmaker?"

She tossed him a glance, accompanied by raised eyebrows. "From the look of things last night, I don't need to."

The comment was casual enough, but he saw something in her eyes. A hint of pain, or maybe disappointment. It bothered him to think he'd hurt her or let her down. He needed to explain. "I assume you saw us kissing."

Effie's gaze went back to the road ahead, only a slight stiffening of her shoulders showing the effect of his words. "I wasn't spying on you," she said. "I'm glad everything's working out all right. I always felt the two of you were meant for each other."

"Effie, I'm in no position to get involved with anyone right now. Not your sister or you." He frowned, suddenly aware of how involved he was already. That he cared what Effie thought proved his involvement with her.

Her look turned serious. Concerned. "Because of your heart? Or rather, that stress attack?"

"In a way." It was what had triggered everything. "I have some major decisions to make in the next few months. Decisions about my store and my life."

"And there's no room in your life for a woman?" She slowed the car as they neared the grocery store's parking lot.

"No." At least he hadn't thought so. Not until two days ago.

"Bernadette would be good for you."

She said it so sincerely, Parker smiled. "And you wouldn't be?"

"No, I wouldn't." Switching off the car, she released her seat belt and faced him. "I can't imagine a worse combination than you and me. Talk about mismatched couples. I . . . we—"

She didn't finish. Shaking her head, she opened her door. "Make sure Mopsy doesn't get out."

For someone so small, Effie moved with a speed and agility that amazed Parker. She was nearly to the store's automatic door by the time he caught up with her. "I thought you and I got along pretty well Friday night. Especially after dinner, when we were in my car."

She shot him a quick scowl and headed for the carts.

"Whether it should be or not," he called after her, "there's something going on between us."

She faced him, still scowling. "And nothing was going on between you and Bernadette last night?"

To say he'd kissed Bernadette because he'd been curious would sound callous, yet he couldn't tell Effie that he'd needed to prove to himself that it wasn't simply hormones going wild that excited him whenever he was around her. "I like Bernadette," he admitted. "I always have. But—"

Effie didn't let him finish. "Give it a chance. Get to know her again. Bern is a smart woman, and she's got a lot to offer a man. Maybe she can help you make these decisions you're facing."

Another rumble of thunder, loud enough to vibrate the building, rolled across the sky. Effie glanced at the windows facing the parking lot. Drops of rain, as big as puddles, were starting to fall. "We'd better get this stuff and get back to the car. I cracked the windows for Mopsy. If the wind picks up, my car will be soaked."

They split the list and were through the checkout lane in less than ten minutes. Rain was falling heavily when they dashed for the car, each carrying a bag. Mopsy greeted them with excited barks and a wagging tail, jumping between the front seat and back. By the time Effie had the car started, it was a downpour, the wipers futilely slapping back and forth. The motor running, she waited, knowing the storm would pass as quickly as it had come. The tension within her, however, would not leave.

She glanced Parker's way, then back out through the windshield. He was watching her, staring at her with those piercing blue eyes of his. "What?" she asked nervously, the closeness of the car getting to her.

"What 'what'?" he asked with a smile in his voice.

She refused to look at him again. "Don't stare at me."

"Why not? I like looking at you. You're a very attractive woman."

"I'm a shrimp, remember."

"An adorable shrimp. Smile."

She didn't smile. "Why?"

"Because I like to see your cheeks dimple."

She gave him a quick, artificial smile, then switched on the defroster to clear the windows.

"Ever think it would get this steamy between us?" he asked.

"It's all the hot air you're spewing," she said, but remembered how many times she had imagined them in steamier situations. The thought caused a tightening deep within her body. "I thought you were the man who didn't want to get involved with anyone?"

"What you want and what happens aren't always the same."

"And now you're going to tell me I'm irresistible?" She did look at him then, certain he was teasing her. The seriousness of his expression bothered her. Quickly, she looked forward again.

"I don't know what's going on," he said.

Neither did she.

"I'd like to explore it," he added.

Explorations often didn't show any results, Effie thought. Her father had told her that once, when he'd talked about his disappointments at various digs. Effie had understood. Life had tossed her a disappointment or two. The loss of her mother. A father who was never there when she needed him. Men who touched her heart and then disappeared.

She didn't need any more disappointments.

Effie put the car into gear. "It's let up a little. I think we'd better get back to Bern."

SEVEN

Effie dropped off the supplies at the cottage. She also dropped off Parker, and before he or Bern could think of any more ways to complicate her life, she took off, found one of her high-school friends, and for two hours caught up on all that had happened since her last visit. By the time she returned to the cottage, the rain had stopped and the sky was clearing.

The storm had eased the humidity level, but not the heat, and Effie wasn't surprised to find Parker and Bernadette in the water. "Come on in!" he called to her as she left her car.

Mopsy ran down to the water's edge, barking. The small dog put her front feet in, then backed up and barked again. Effie noticed that Bernadette smiled and shaded her eyes with her hand, but didn't ask her to join them.

Not that it mattered. Effie had no intention of turning a twosome into a threesome. "I need to get back to work," she called to them. "I've done my sloughing off for the day."

"Water's great," Parker said to entice her.

She was sure it was. In July, the water temperature was usually in the seventies. Almost bathwater. It was hard to believe that six months from now ice fishermen would be driving their cars out onto the lake. Not that the practice was wise. Snowmobilers had lost their lives by overestimating the thickness of the ice.

The danger now, as far as Effie was concerned, was Parker. She could tell herself he was off-limits, and there might be a little more flesh on his body than when he'd been in college, but he still had an appeal she couldn't ignore. Except, she had to ignore it.

"I'll take a dip later," she said, then called to Mopsy and headed for the back door.

Effie had everything pulled out of the hall closet and spread over the worn living-room carpet when Bernadette came into the cottage. Modellike, she dragged her beach towel behind her and strolled closer. Stopping in front of Effie, she sighed dramatically. "What an absolutely perfect afternoon."

From her cross-legged positon on the floor, Effie looked up at her sister. "Things going well, I take it."

"Perfect," Bern repeated, and crouched to scratch Mopsy behind her ears. "Parker's taking me out to dinner. I'm about to convince that man I can make his job easier." She tapped Mopsy on the nose. "What do you think about that, puppy dog?"

"Sounds like things are going *very* well," Effie said, hoping she sounded more enthusiastic than she felt.

"He said to ask you if you wanted to join us." Head cocked, Bern rose to her feet. "Seems to me he's showing quite an interest in you."

"Me?" Effie heard the squeak in her voice and hurried to control it. "Don't be silly. He still calls me shrimp. To him, I'm just your little sister."

"There you go, underestimating your appeal. For a shrimp, you're one cute kid."

"But men like Parker aren't interested in kids." She looked up at Bernadette. Her sister's midnight-blue swimsuit emphasized the slimness of her body and the curves of her breasts, while her legs seemed to go on forever. Even after a swim, Bern looked as if she'd stepped out of a fashion magazine. "It's women like you who interest men like him. Not women who clown around."

"From what he said to me earlier, I wouldn't be so sure of that. Consider how eager he was to go shopping with you. And he was disappointed when you didn't come swimming."

"Oh, right." Effie wouldn't—couldn't—allow herself to consider the possibility that Parker felt for her what she felt for him, and the last thing she wanted was to make her sister jealous. "Come on, Bern. He was being friendly, that's all. He's not my type. He's too serious."

"And you're not?"

"You know what I mean."

A shake of her head swung Bernadette's hair across her shoulders. "I know when it comes to men, you're even pickier than I am. Beats me how you're ever going to find one who will satisfy all your criteria."

"I'm not all that picky," Effie argued. "I just want a man who's dependable."

"And you don't think Parker is?"

Effie remembered back to the night, thirteen years ago, when he'd kissed her. He'd fired her dreams that night, had given her hope. Then he'd taken off. Just two nights ago, he'd rekindled those dreams. Now he was playing her off Bernadette. "I think you're the one who will find out."

Bern smiled. "I do have a feeling I'm going to be spending a lot of time with him."

Effie was in bed, but not asleep when Bernadette returned that night. She knew exactly when Bern stepped into the room they'd shared for so many years. Without turning on a light, Bern crossed over to sit on the side of the bed that had been hers. Mopsy left her spot by Effie's side and went to her.

"You awake?" Bernadette asked in a loud whisper.

Effie groaned, as if disturbed, and shifted under the sheet, but didn't answer. Not that it mattered. Bernadette went on.

"I'm going to have to go back to Chicago tomorrow."

"To Chicago?" Effie sat up.

"I need to talk to some people, make some decisions."

"What about the cottage? We need to have things ready by Friday." Not that the cottage was the problem. The problem was Parker. With Bern gone, all of his lethal sex appeal would be directed at her. She didn't trust herself around him.

"We'll have everything ready by Friday." Bern switched her pats from Mopsy's head to Effie's arm. "We got a lot done today, and I'll be back sometime Tuesday. I promise. Also, Parker said he'd come over tomorrow and give you a hand."

Effie groaned again. "I don't want Parker helping me. Why do you have to go?"

Bernadette chuckled. "You sound just like you did

when I told you I was going away to college. 'Why do you have to go?' you whined back then."

"I'm not whining, and this is different."

Bernadette continued patting her arm. "Trust me. You won't even know I'm gone."

The moment she opened her eyes the next morning, Effie knew Bernadette was gone. It was a feeling at first, then a reality when she found the note Bern had left on the kitchen table. *Be back tomorrow. Love, Bern,* was all it said. Effie numbly stared at the piece of paper.

Be back tomorrow.

But what about today? She didn't want Parker coming over, didn't want his help. When she was around him, she felt all tingly, eager, hopeful. Just the sight of him made her want what she couldn't have.

Maybe he could play games, but she couldn't. Not this type of game. If he wanted Bern, fine; that was as it should be. But every time he looked at her with those blue eyes of his, every time he touched her, kissed her . . .

It was more than she could take.

Effie didn't accomplish much in the next few hours. She didn't want Parker to come over, but when he didn't stop by, she was upset. Every time she passed a window that faced his cottage, she checked for movement, for some sign of his presence. Nothing. She couldn't concentrate on any one project and kept switching, first continuing her work on the hall closet, then going to the dining room, then to her room.

Her old clown posters still hung on the walls, and a clown lamp still sat on the old dresser she'd used as a child. On shelves her grandfather had built were various-sized statues of clowns, many bought for her by her grandmother. Every time Effie stepped into the room, they triggered memories of a promise unfulfilled. She didn't want to keep them, none of them, not even for atmosphere in the shop. They represented failure. Out of sight; out of mind. It seemed the best way to go. Friday, she would put them out to sell.

The rhythmic putt of a boat's motor, clearly close to shore, tore her thoughts from the past. Leaving her bedroom, Effie checked through the window facing the lake. She could just barely see Parker mooring his pontoon boat at his dock. Her question why he hadn't come over was answered. He'd been fishing. Fishing while she was fretting.

He stepped onto the dock and tied up his boat, then systematically began unloading it. From a distance, she could daydream without guilt, covet without fear of anyone knowing. To his face, she might deny any interest, but in her heart she knew it would always be there. More than mere physical appeal, something about Parker touched her. As different as they were, there'd always been a kinship between them. He was like a friend whom you didn't see for a long time, then met again to find you could pick up the friendship as if you'd never been apart. He made her feel whole. He made her feel alive. With Parker, there would always be a spark. Young or old, in his prime or his dotage, he would always be her knight in shining armor.

He dropped his fishing poles, and they hit the dock with a clatter. Mopsy barked, and Parker looked toward her cottage.

Immediately, she pulled back from the window and out of sight. What she'd been thinking was idiotic. Here she was, wasting her time mooning over a man she didn't even want. Well, shouldn't want.

Grumbling to herself, she turned back to her room.

The sun was high above when Parker pulled the assortment of boxes he'd picked up at the grocers out of his car and headed for Effie's cottage. A deerfly began circling his head, and he swatted at it with a box, then used the side of his arm to rub away the perspiration on his forehead. Packing and getting ready for a yard sale were not high on his list of things he wanted to do when the temperature hovered around ninety and the humidity was as high, but it was an excuse to be around Effie. As much as he'd told himself the timing was all wrong, he did want to see her again. At her screen door, he shifted the boxes and knocked with his elbow.

Mopsy came tearing out of the bedroom, barking excitedly. Effie followed more slowly. Even through the screen, her guarded expression and stiff posture were evident. Parker wiggled past her when she opened the door, the boxes he carried bumping the sides of the doorway. "I don't know if this is enough," he said, setting them on the floor. "But the store manager said we could get more if we needed them."

"These will help." Effie stayed her distance as Mopsy sniffed at the boxes.

"He also said we could borrow a pricing gun." Again, Parker swiped at the perspiration on his forehead. "It's another stinker. Where do you want me to start?"

"Nowhere. I mean, I appreciate your getting the boxes, but I can handle things here. You're supposed to be on a vacation—relaxing."

"I relaxed this morning. I went fishing. Not that I

caught anything. I did see Bern. She wasn't kidding when she said she was going to take off early."

"I never heard her leave."

"She said you were still asleep." He grinned his wickedest grin. "I was tempted to come over and wake you."

Effie grunted a response, her look suspicious.

"So?" He glanced toward the living room. "Do you want me to finish in there? I think we got the books all sorted yesterday, but we didn't touch the VCR tapes."

"I took care of those." She stayed by the door. "Maybe you should go get more boxes. You can never have enough boxes, you know."

What he knew was that Effie wanted him gone. And if he were wise, he would take the hint, bring some more boxes, and get out of her life. He certainly hadn't been relaxing lately. In the last three and a half days, he'd been physically aroused, physically exhausted, and mentally stimulated. It was wonderful.

Leaving, however, wasn't an option he wanted to consider. How could he when she looked so damned appealing, her feet bare and her body barely covered by gym shorts and a tank top, her cheeks flushed from the heat, her curls damp against her skin, and a brightness to her eyes he couldn't ignore? By reputation, redheads had fiery tempers; he was more interested in Effie's fiery passion. No, he couldn't walk away, not this time.

He stepped toward her, crowding her, and enjoyed the flash of awareness that streaked through her eyes. *"We'll* get the boxes later," he said softly.

"But—"

He cut her short. Grasping her shoulders, he drew her close and covered her mouth with his. He didn't want reasons why they shouldn't be together. He'd given himself enough reasons to last a lifetime. Reasons didn't matter when the briefest of her smiles could warm him from the inside out and holding her felt so right.

He expected her to resist, and for a moment she did, her body unyielding. Then she groaned, and the resistance was gone, her lips blending with his. She gave even as she received, her mouth soft and warm against his.

Her refusal to acknowledge the attraction between them had irked him, but her submission was far more dangerous. Needs too long suppressed demanded satisfaction. A kiss would not be enough. He wanted to know her, to hold and possess, to claim and be claimed. Sliding his hands down her back, he pressed her hips to his, leaving no question of his desire.

Again, she groaned, the sound a plaintive cry for more, and the heat within him intensified. Only when the resistance returned, her hands going to his shoulders, pushing as she stepped back, did he stop kissing her.

"I—we—" She pulled away, shaking her head, the bounce of her auburn curls giving emphasis to her denial. "I think you'd better leave."

"No."

Her eyes relayed her surprise. As quickly, she frowned. "I don't know what kind of game you're playing, Parker Morgan, but I don't go around making out with my sister's boyfriend the moment she leaves town."

"That was more than making out, and I am not your sister's boyfriend. Not anymore. That was thirteen years ago, Effie."

"That's not what she thinks. And why would she? Ever since she arrived, you've been together."

"Because you've wanted it that way. You're the one who was all ready to leave me with her Friday night, who took off yesterday afternoon, who wouldn't join us for a swim or dinner."

"Because I don't interfere with my sister's love affairs."

"And if I were involved with your sister, I'd consider that quite noble."

She lifted her chin, looking him straight in the eyes. "She thinks you're involved."

"Is that what she said?"

"Yes."

"Then there's been a misunderstanding."

For a moment she said nothing, just kept looking at him. Finally, she turned her head away. "Well, it doesn't matter. I'm not interested in your games."

"I'm not playing games."

"You know what I mean." She started down the short hallway to the bedrooms. "If you're determined to do something, you could go through the things in the shed. I don't think anything's been touched since Grandpa died. There's a lot of fishing gear and tools. Much of it's as ancient as Grandpa was. Take anything you want, and with the rest, decide if we should sell it or just toss it. I wouldn't know."

She was determined to get him out of the house. Well, he would leave for now, do as she'd asked. But he wasn't going to let her ignore her feelings. "You may not be interested in games, but you are interested," he said firmly. "Just remember that."

How could she forget? Effie had him out of the house, but not out of her mind. For the next hour, no matter where she worked in the cottage, she was aware of where he was. The hum of the floor fan in her bedroom didn't cover the clanking and banging going on in the shed, no more than the air the fan blew over her cooled the memory of his kisses or the need he'd tempted. She was interested all right. Too damned interested.

The screen door slammed, and she flinched, then tensed. He was in the cottage. Holding her breath, she waited for him to call out or come down the hallway. Mopsy trotted out of the room to investigate, and Effie heard Parker speak to the dog, his smooth baritone doing nothing to soothe her taut nerves.

A minute went by, then two. She held her breath, yet neither Parker nor Mopsy appeared in the doorway.

Go away, she willed him, afraid her resistance would be nil. Call it quits. I'm not interested.

Liar, her subconscious yelled.

Closing her eyes, she shook her head. What was Parker doing to her? Driving her crazy. And why did Bern have to go and take off for Chicago? Loyalty and nobleness were all fine and dandy, but how noble could one be when faced with such temptation?

Under her breath, she swore at her sister.

"My, my. I didn't know you knew those words."

Effie snapped her eyes open. Parker stood in the doorway, a tall glass of lemonade in each hand. "I don't know about you," he said, stepping into the room, "but I am melting out in that shed." He stopped in front of the fan. "At least you have this."

"I told you, you don't have to help."

"You've told me a lot of things." He held one glass toward her. "I think we need to talk."

"About what?" She took the glass he offered, but didn't rise from the floor. Warily, she kept watch of him.

"About us." He walked over to the bed and sat on the end. Drinking from his own glass, he looked around the room. "What are you going to do with the clown posters?"

"Sell them, if anyone wants them. Or throw them away." She didn't want to talk about posters. "Parker, this is crazy. There is no us. I'm not your type."

"And what is my type?"

"Bern."

"If that's so, why am I attracted to you?"

"I don't know." Undoubtedly there was a rational reason. "Maybe because you had that attack. Your doctors told you to relax, and because you and I used to kid around, you see me as a means to relax."

His laugh was short and cryptic, and he glanced down at the front of his shorts. "Relaxing is not what I've been doing around you."

She understood his meaning, and perhaps that was part of the problem. "When was the last time you were with a woman?"

"Months ago. Don't worry. I have no diseases. That was one of the many tests they ran while I was in the hospital."

"I wasn't worried." She hadn't even thought about it. "But I'm sure Bern will be glad to know that."

He shook his head, smiling. "When are you going to realize it's not Bern but you who, so to speak, raises my interest?"

"But—"

"Trust me, it was as much a surprise to me as it is to you." He set his glass on the lamp table by her bed. "But the timing's all wrong. I came here to relax, make some decisions about the store. I didn't come to the lake to get involved with you."

He made it sound as if it were her fault, and that irked her. "So get uninvolved. I haven't encouraged you."

He smiled wryly. "Anything but."

"You've got decisions to make? Well, so do I. I co-own a business that features 'clowns for hire' as part of its draw, and I can't even put on a clown suit."

"And I have to decide if I should sell Morgan's Department Stores." He stood and walked to the window. "We both have problems."

She stared at his back. "You're thinking of selling the stores?"

He glanced at her. "I've had an offer. A major company is interested. All I have to do is say yes, and I'm out of the business. No more stress, no more worries."

"That's wonderful."

"Is it?" He shrugged and looked back out the window. "Don't forget, I grew up constantly hearing how my grandfather started Morgan's and how my father expanded it. We're talking about a family legacy. How do you sell a legacy?"

"A legacy that killed your father and is killing you."

"Maybe that's part of the legacy."

"Bull." She couldn't believe he'd said that. "Parker, I remember a night thirteen years ago when you told me you didn't want anything to do with the business. You wanted to major in English. Become a writer. You were ready to turn your back on the family legacy that night."

"And you said, 'Do it, if that's what you want.'"

"But you didn't."

"Ah, that's the problem. I did. The very next day, I headed for New York City, and for two years, I ignored the family legacy and wrote the great American novel."

"You did what?" She couldn't believe it. His story didn't fit what she knew.

"The day after I practically raped you on the dock, I left for New York. For two years, I turned my back on everything I'd been raised to become. I did pursue my dreams. Selfishly did exactly what I wanted. And then I got a call from my mother. My father was dead."

"But she told me . . ." Effie clearly remembered her conversation with Ruth Morgan. "Your mother told me you'd gone back to college."

He shook his head. "She's always been in denial. If life doesn't exactly fit her dreamworld, she makes things up. I've even caught her telling people I graduated from the University of Michigan."

"You didn't?"

"Nope." He grinned. "You're looking at a college dropout."

"So drop out of the business world."

"And do what?"

"Finish writing that great American novel. You should get enough money selling the stores to follow that dream."

He shook his head. "Some dreams die natural deaths. The publishers who saw what I had written didn't think it was that great. Besides, selling the stores involves others. I'm no longer a self-centered twenty-year-old thinking only of my own wants. I've seen what my actions can cause. My father's dead, and I have my mother to consider. She still owns a share of the business. What I do will affect her. Also, I have employees who depend on me."

"And if you drop dead, what will they do? What will your mother do?"

She could tell from his frown that he didn't like her bringing that up. He looked away. "Bernadette's trying to convince me she's my salvation."

"As your wife?"

"No. As a general manager of the stores."

Effie could see Bernadette in that position. "Are you going to hire her?"

"We're discussing it." Pushing himself away from the window, he started toward her. "So, you see, the relationship I have with Bern is strictly business. Whereas the relationship I want to have with you . . ."

Effie scooted to her feet. "Parker, I think we need to get back to work."

His smile was rakish. "It's too hot to work."

She moved toward the door in an attempt to keep them apart. His hand snaked out to catch her arm, but she avoided it.

"Another of those tai chi moves?" he asked.

"No, I learned that in elementary school, on the playground." She knew she couldn't keep avoiding him. A quick exit was her safest bet. "Actually, you're right, it is too hot to work. I think this would be a good time for me to stop by and see Cindy's little girl."

"Good idea." He grinned. "I'll go with you."

EIGHT

"Effie. Parker. What a surprise." Cindy's greeting was as warm as the day. "And who is this?" She reached out to pat Mopsy on the head.

Mopsy, from her position under Effie's arm, licked Cindy's hand, and Effie introduced them. "We came to see your daughter."

"You couldn't have come at a better time." Cindy's smile disappeared. "Mandy's not having a very good day. Maybe company will help."

She ushered them through the large ranch house, taking a moment to reintroduce them to her mother. Mrs. Keyser gushed over Parker. Effie had a feeling all women did. Mopsy got the usual pat on the head and baby talk, and Effie was reminded that she hadn't grown an inch.

"Just call me a shrimp," she responded, glancing at Parker.

He showed no remorse in his use of the nickname, simply grinned. They didn't get that much from Amanda Nelson when Cindy introduced them. The child barely lifted her head from the pillow on the sofa in the den. That was, until she saw Mopsy. "You have a dog?"

"This is Mopsy." Effie moved closer and crouched in front of the sofa.

Mandy reached out with a thin, frail hand and stroked Mopsy's long hair, and Effie understood Cindy's concern. Though Mandy wore a colorful shorts outfit, the bright pinks and yellows merely accentuated the child's paleness. She looked as though a strong wind would blow her away, and only her large blue eyes showed any life.

"Can she do tricks?" Mandy asked shyly."

"Dozens." Effie stood and set Mopsy on the carpeting. "If it's all right with your mother, Mopsy would like to entertain you."

Both Mandy and Effie glanced at Cindy, and Cindy nodded.

"Have you ever seen a dog dance?" Effie asked Mandy.

"Dance? No." With an effort, Mandy pushed herself to a sitting position. Immediately, Cindy was by her daughter's side, fluffing the pillow and fussing over her.

Effie started to move the coffee table to make room for Mopsy to perform, but Parker took over, shifting furniture here and there. He worked with efficiency, leaving her little to do except watch. But then, watching him had always been a pleasure. Every step he took commanded her attention; every smile melted away more of her resistance. She'd hoped to escape him by saying she was going to Cindy's. Instead, here she was about to put on a show for him.

Then again, she thought, maybe that was a good thing. The next few minutes should open his eyes. Watching her act like an idiot would no doubt clarify in his mind which sister he wanted.

Once an area was cleared and Mandy was ready, Effie pulled out a wooden whistle. Immediately Mopsy came alert.

Parker stood back by the wall and out of the way, watching as Effie blew a tune of sorts through the whistle, her cheeks puffing out. Mopsy danced about on her hind legs, and Mandy laughed, a hint of color reaching her cheeks.

His glance moved to Cindy. She was watching her daughter, love and anguish clearly written on her face. Thirteen years ago, he would have classified Cindy as an airhead. Time had changed more than her physical appearance. The eighteen-year-old copycat of Bernadette had matured beyond her thirty-one years. He could understand her desire to help her child. Even he was touched by Mandy's fragile smiles.

He was also touched by Effie. She knelt in front of Mandy and circled her arms so Mopsy could jump through them, then she bent over so Mopsy could hop on her back. Once the dog was in place, Effie looked about as if she'd lost Mopsy, and Mandy laughed and pointed. Effie pretended not to understand, turning here and there, as if following Mandy's directions.

Even without the makeup and baggy clothes, Effie was the clown. She'd always been the clown, the one to turn a serious matter funny. He remembered how she would exaggerate a situation until he could see the humorous side. He'd thought her a child back then, incapable of understanding how serious his problems were, and her mockery had sometimes irritated him. What he hadn't realized was how much clearer her teasing and jokes had made his problems appear. How easy to miss the gift of the comic.

Effie continued playing the fool, looking for her dog. She had a sick child's complete attention.

She had his complete attention.

She "discovered" Mopsy on her back and did a pirouette, then began walking across the room, Mopsy darting between her legs. Hers was a ballet of slapstick, each trick choreographed to perfection, right up to the end. Mopsy jumped, and Effie caught her in midair. "This is where she always jumped into my pocket," she explained to Mandy, then set the dog back down on the carpet. "That was when I was still a clown."

"What do you mean 'when'?" Cindy asked, patting her daughter's shoulder. "She's still a clown, isn't she, Mandy, honey?"

Mandy's eyes sparkled with awe. "Are you really a clown?"

"Was."

"Do you have a big red nose or a little red nose?"

For a moment Parker wasn't sure if Effie would answer, then she smiled at Mandy and used her hands to exaggerate a bulbous nose. "Bigger than big."

"And a white face?"

"With a great big smile." Effie reached out and drew a smile on Mandy's face. "Just like that."

"I want to be a clown when I grow up. Will you come to my birthday party?" Mandy looked up at her mother. "Could she, please?"

"Of course she can, honey." Cindy trained a pleading look on Effie. "It's just going to be family."

The laughter once again left Effie's face, her mouth closing in on a straight line. "I'm sorry, I can't."

"Please," Mandy begged.

"I would, but—" Effie shook her head, stepping back, and Parker moved to her side. She looked up at him. "I can't."

He knew the memories she held and repeated her statement. "Effie can't do it right now. She would like to, but she can't. We're glad we got to meet you, Mandy. Now we've got to be going."

"Yes." Effie quickly picked up on his comment. "We've got to be going. I still have a lot to do at the cottage. Come on, Mopsy. Good-bye, Mandy. You get well, okay?"

Mandy gave a weak reply, and Effie scooped up Mopsy and hurried out of the room. Parker followed her, but Cindy stopped them before they reached the front door. "Come here. I want to show you something."

She led them to a bedroom. Mandy's bedroom, Parker was sure. The child's toys were everywhere. One glance, and he knew why Cindy had brought them there. So much about the room reminded him of Effie's room at the cottage: the clown posters on the walls and the clown statues on her dresser.

"She's just like you used to be," Cindy told Effie. "She wants everything and anything to do with clowns. If you can't come for her birthday, maybe another time. It would mean so much. You made her laugh today. She hasn't laughed in so long."

"It was Mopsy who made her laugh." Effie stepped back, away from the reminders of what she'd once loved. "If you want a clown, I'm sure my partner, Joan, would come. She does a lot with balloons and is good for parties."

Cindy placed a hand on Effie's arm. "Why not you? She really liked you. You and Mopsy. I know I give in to her too much, but I just want her to get better."

"I know you do." Effie hugged Cindy. "I'll have Joan call you. Mandy will like her just as much as she liked me. I know she will. I would do it if . . . if I—"

Parker saw the tears in Effie's eyes and said their good-byes. He didn't push for conversation until they were driving away from Cindy's. Even then, he started out casual. "That's a cute act you have with Mopsy. I imagine it's really funny when you're in costume."

She glanced his way, her expression mildly suspicious. "It always got a lot of laughs."

He decided to go for the bottom line. "How is it you could do it today, but you don't feel you can do it for her birthday party?"

"She wants a clown, Parker. The makeup and the costume. It makes a difference."

"How? Why?"

For someone who didn't know, Effie guessed those were logical questions. "When you're in costume, you are no longer you. You're whatever persona you've chosen to be. Me, I was Effie the Effervescent. The big painted smile, the exaggerated eyes with sparkles, and the huge, shiny red nose. I wore a baggy costume with sparkles all over and big baggy pockets. I had the over-sized shoes. I was the typical 'Auguste' clown."

"A goose?"

"No." She spelled it for him. "There are basically three types of clowns nowadays. The white face, the Auguste, and the hobo. There used to be national clowns, those who poked fun at the different nationalities, but that's no longer politically correct. Probably one of the most famous Auguste clowns ever was Emmett Kelly. The Auguste is the straight man, the fool."

"Which you were today with Mopsy."

Effie stroked Mopsy's head. "Children love seeing her outwit me."

"You play the fool well. And I guess I'm dumb, but I still don't understand why, if you could do the tricks with her, you can't be a clown?"

Looking out the side window, Effie remembered another man who hadn't understood. She'd tried to explain it to Kent. She would try with Parker. "Being a clown is more than just putting on a costume and makeup. It's a whole way of thinking, a way of acting. When I'm a clown, I can't eat, drink, chew gum, or swear. All of my skin must be covered, either with makeup or clothing. Effie Sanders ceases to exist, and Effie the Effervescent takes over."

"And Effie the Effervescent is refusing to come out and play."

"I know it sounds crazy." It did to her, yet she couldn't rationalize the feelings away. "I have tried to put on the makeup and costume. I just can't do it."

"I believe you." He continued driving around the lake toward England Point. "Tell me more about being a clown."

"Like what?"

"Like how do you decide what you're going to look like?"

"Well, when I went to clown school, they stressed that even if we weren't in the circus, we were professionals and this should be reflected in our appearance. No cheap wigs or shoddy clothing. Not that you have to pay a fortune for an outfit. I found my trousers and shirt at the Goodwill. What's important is you should look like you care about your appearance. Actually, I found deciding what my face would look like the most difficult part. No two clown faces can be the same. There's only one Emmett Kelly. One Coco. One Lou Jacobs. Only one Effie the Effervescent."

"Sounds more complicated than I'd imagined. Lots of dos and don'ts."

"Clowns take their work very seriously."

He chuckled, and she realized what she'd said. "Now there's a paradox, but I am serious. We have an image to uphold. One that's very old. Clowns go back to at least the beginning of the nineteen century, and even further if you think of the fools and jesters of the Middle Ages and the Renaissance."

"And how far back do you go? When did Effie Sanders become Effie the Effervescent?"

"I went to clown school six years ago, but you remember how I wanted to be a clown. I fell in love with the clowns the first time Grandma and Grandpa took me to the circus, and I picked the name when I was in seventh grade. Effervescent was on our spelling list."

"So for all those years, you wanted to be a clown, and now you're through being a clown. The dream's gone"—he snapped his fingers—"just like that?"

"It's not that the dream's gone. I—I just can't do it."

"Effie, I know you feel bad about letting your grandmother down, but what about Mandy? By giving up clowning, you're letting her down, aren't you?"

She closed her eyes, his question too painful to answer.

After a moment she felt him pull the car to the side of the road and stop, and she opened her eyes and looked at him. He was studying her, his penetrating gaze making her uneasy. "What?"

" 'What?' is a good question." He shook his head. "What am I going to do with you?"

"You don't need to do anything." She looked away. "I'm fine."

"Are you?"

"I just need some time." She bit her lower lip, knowing she needed more than time. She needed her grandmother back.

"Effie, she loved you. I'm sure she understood."

"How could she understand?" Tears blurred her vision, and Effie tried to squeeze them away. "I don't understand. All I know is I let her down."

"You didn't mean to."

"That doesn't matter. For all of my life, I've heard my father make excuses for missing important events. 'I didn't mean to. I'm sorry,' he always says. I swore I would never be like him, but I am. I'm just like him. I missed the most important event in my grandmother's life, her dying. Being sorry will never change that."

"So you carry the guilt around, wishing you could turn back the clock and do it all over again? Do things different?" Instead of sympathy, he scoffed. "Come on, Effie. You're not alone in this guilt business. I have it. I ask myself, over and over, what if I hadn't gone to New York? What if I had done as my parents wanted: finished school, gone into the business when I graduated, helped my father, and eased his workload? Would he still be alive today?"

"I share your guilt there." He should see that, she thought. He probably blamed her. "After all, I was the one who kept telling you to follow your dreams."

"Because I kept telling you I didn't want to major in business, that I wanted to live in Greenwich Village, experience life, and write. You didn't initiate the idea." He chuckled, but the sound held no mirth. "You were probably sick and tired of hearing me go on and on about it."

"You had your dreams, and I had mine. Now you've abandoned yours, and I can't follow mine. We're a great pair."

"That's what I keep telling you." Leaning close, he brushed his lips against hers. "We're a great pair."

Light and spontaneous, his kiss surprised Effie. She stared at him wide-eyed, knowing she should say something, that he hadn't understood. How could he and still think her worthy?

The words didn't come when his hands touched her

face, caressing her cheeks. He leaned toward her again, and her heart did a flip. Her mind yelled, *Pull back*.

She leaned toward him.

"You were wonderful with Mandy," he said. "Thank you for letting me watch."

His words were butter soft, his look melting. Her mind spun in confusion. "I thought you would—"

He didn't let her finish. Once more his mouth covered hers. His lips playing over her carried messages of assurance. He hadn't found her act silly. He didn't think her selfish and shallow. He was thanking her.

The taste of him and the warmth of his lips became salves to her guilt, cleansing it away. Later there would be new guilts. New condemnations. Later she would think about her sister, but right now, with his tongue sliding into her mouth and a jolt of need shooting through her, all Effie thought about was wanting him.

The honk of a horn from a passing car jarred her back to reality. With a gasp, she pulled away. "Parker?"

His smile showed only pleasure, no remorse. "What?"

"Why did you do that?"

"Because I like kissing you. Because afterward, I always wonder if kissing you was really as wonderful as I remember."

"And?" For her, kissing him had her standing on her head. Laughing. Crying. Juggling dozens of emotions. Had her mind doing cartwheels.

His smile became smug. "There's nothing wrong with my memory."

"This is crazy."

"I agree."

Crazy and wonderful. "I think we'd better get going." She needed time to think and motioned for him to drive on. "This isn't the way things were supposed to happen. You're supposed to be with Bern."

"So you keep saying. But life, I'm discovering, is full of surprises."

As a clown, she'd used the element of surprise to her advantage. Parker had her at a disadvantage. "For thirteen years, I don't see you except for some televison ads, then suddenly you pop back into my life, and start kissing me and sweet-talking me. It doesn't make sense."

"That or it makes very good sense." He slowed at an intersection, then turned right. "Not seeing you for thirteen years was my fault. There were times I thought about you, and I could have written, but I never knew what to say. When I left here, I had so many dreams. I pictured myself on the best-seller lists, touring the country for book promotions." He laughed. "Oh the dreams I had."

She remembered. He'd shared them with her often enough. His parents had seen only a model son. If his dreams weren't theirs, they didn't want to hear them. So he'd told her. And she'd told him to follow them.

She'd never expected him to actually do it. "Tell me everything that happened after you left me that night."

"Everything?" He grinned. "Well, first off, I had an argument with my parents. I'd had it with their demands. The next day, while they were playing golf, I drew out all of the money I had in my savings account, packed my bags, and headed for New York City. I was going to show them."

"You found a place in Greenwich Village?"

"Close enough. For two years, I lived on West Fifty-seventh, on the fifth floor of an apartment building where the elevator was always breaking down. I shared three rooms with two others, each of us dreaming of becoming famous. Joe and Katherine were going to be in the theater. I, of course, was going to write that great American novel. We were poor and happy."

"Did any of you succeed?"

He shrugged. "I suppose it depends on your definition of 'succeed.' Over the years, Katherine has gotten a few good parts. Most are off Broadway, but the reviews she's sent have been great."

"And the other guy?"

"Joe gave up and is selling insurance. And I, of course, after my mother's call, went back to the business I was supposed to take over from the beginning. Back to my destiny."

She heard the remorse. His dream had gone unfulfilled. "What did you do with your book?"

"Put it in a closet. I did pull it out last month and read parts." He wrinkled his nose. "It was bad."

"Sez you."

"Trust me. It is bad." He glanced her way. "Do you really need to get back to the cottage, or would you have time for an ice-cream cone?"

"A Curly Cone cone?"

He picked butter pecan, she asked for chocolate, and bought vanilla for Mopsy. They sat outside the Curly Cone Drive-in, at a table with an umbrella for shade. Effie held Mopsy's cone in one hand, letting the dog lick at it, and her own cone in her other hand. On the road in front of them, cars drove by, those going west heading toward Grand Rapids, those facing east bound for the park or Yankee Springs or any number of destinations. Watching Effie lick at the chocolate river running down the side of her cone, Parker wondered what their destinations would be.

"I remember taking you and Bernadette out for ice cream," he said. "You always got more on you than in."

"It's the heat. I can't keep up with it."

At the moment it was also because she was trying to feed her dog at the same time she was eating hers. Mopsy got another lick, and another rivulet ran down the side of Effie's cone. With the flick of her tongue, she stopped it. The action caused a tightening in his loins, and he suppressed a groan.

He couldn't seem to get his mind off Effie and her body. He'd never let hormones rule him before. It bothered him now.

Effie picked up the conversation. "You know, in the few years I've been away, this place has already changed. New homes." She laughed. "New canals to the lake. They're going to create as much shoreline as they can."

"Lakefront property brings the money. You should get a good price for your grandmother's place."

"I'd keep it if I could afford it."

He heard her sigh, and looked back at her. Again, she was losing her battle with the ice cream, two streams running down the cone. Diligently she battled each. Between licks, she continued. "I'm surprised you held on to your place."

"It's been a good investment. When it's not rented out, I've let friends use it. Actually, I was lucky to be able to come these two weeks. The place was booked solid this month, but the people who had it for these two weeks canceled at the last minute." He smiled, the irony hitting him. "Almost makes you wonder, doesn't it? Quite a coincidence that I'm here when you're here."

"And when Bern is here."

"When both of you are here." If she wanted it that way, fine. Bern, however, wasn't the one who had him tied in knots.

Some of the chocolate dripped down Effie's chin. He reached across the table, wiping away the ice cream with a napkin. He would have preferred licking it off.

"Bern wouldn't be such a slob," Effie said, a flush of color rising to her cheeks.

"Think of all the fun she misses."

Her cone finished, Mopsy hopped off the bench. Effie told her to stay, but Mopsy ignored her and trotted over to two little girls. Parker laughed. "Your child wants to play."

Sure enough, Mopsy danced around on her hind legs, entertaining the children. Effie went to her dog, but didn't stop her. Instead, when the children asked, Effie had Mopsy do a series of tricks, then answered their questions.

Parker stayed at the table and watched. It wasn't a coincidence that they were at the lake at the same time. It was ironic. For years he'd dated women who fit his image of the perfect mate, and had always found something lacking. Each had been intelligent, sophisticated, and had had that indefinable element called class. But none had held his interest. Now he'd found a woman who did, and she not only didn't fit his preconceived ideas, the timing was all wrong.

He had decisions to make that would affect the rest of his life. He needed time to think. He was supposed to be relaxing, but coming to the lake was taking his mind too far away from the stores. He needed to reevaluate his priorities.

Tossing his napkin and the remains of his cone in the garbage container, he stood and walked over to Effie's side. The girls were petting Mopsy, and Effie was simply watching. "Ready to go?" he asked.

She looked up at him, then down at her dog. This time when she called, Mopsy came.

"It's still too hot to work in that shed," he said as they walked toward his car. "I'll get back to it later."

"Really, you don't have to."

"No problem." He glanced at his watch. "I may drive in to Grand Rapids. See how things are going at the stores."

"You're supposed to be on vacation."

"Old habits die hard."

Effie expected Parker to simply drop her off. Instead, he walked her to the cottage. Before she could open the door, he turned her toward him. "You impressed me today."

"How did I impress you? By acting like a fool for Mandy, or by getting ice cream all over my front?"

The moment she mentioned the ice cream that had dripped onto her top, she wished she hadn't. His gaze dropped to the ribbed white cotton covering her chest. One spot of chocolate lay directly over her nipple, and for a moment her stomach went queasy as she imagined him licking it off.

Instead, he grinned and tousled her hair. "You do get into a cone."

"I got no class."

She said it for a laugh, to ease the tension. Instead, his expression turned serious, his hand going to her chin. He tilted her face up. "You've got plenty of class, Effie Sanders, and don't let anyone tell you otherwise."

"Yes, sir." Joking about it seemed safest. His look was too serious.

His groan was just as serious, a warning she didn't heed. Staring at his mouth, she watched his lips come closer. Automatically, her own parted. If she'd meant to voice a protest, none came out. Her breath locked in her throat, she waited, the beat of her heart sounding in her ears, and a tingle of excitement passing through her.

His kiss brought release, and total involvement. Feigning disinterest was an impossibility, and fighting him off never crossed her mind. She reached out to hold, not to push away.

"Oh, Effie," he murmured against her lips, his breathing already ragged. "I wasn't going to do this."

"I wasn't going to let you do this." From the ice-cream place back, she'd made so many promises to herself. None seemed relevant.

He moved a hand between them, rubbing his palm over first one breast, then the other, with deft expertise. Heat radiated through her top, his caresses creating an ache that traveled deep into her body. Her nipples had become hardened peaks, and when he glanced down at the chocolate-covered one, she knew he was about to put her imagined thoughts into action.

Though his body was shielding them from the lake, there were always children passing through the yard, going from one cottage to the next. "Parker, no." Her warning was breathless. "Someone will see us."

"Then invite me in." His husky voice was an invitation in itself.

She wavered. "We shouldn't."

He moved his hands to cup her bottom, and bent his knees, drawing her hips against his. She felt the hard ridge of his arousal beneath the cotton of his shorts. "You know, I want you."

The words were unnecessary. What was worse, she wanted him. It's wrong, she kept telling herself. Only her body protested her reasoning. Her panties were damp, her legs weak with submission. She didn't want to stop him, wouldn't stop him.

"Damn!" He ground a kiss against her lips, keeping

his body pressed against hers, the contact uninhibitedly intimate. And then he stepped back, releasing her against the screen door, his eyes so dark with passion they were a midnight blue.

"I've got to go," he said, shaking his head as he continued his retreat. "You're right. We shouldn't . . . I shouldn't have. Every time—"

He didn't finish, simply turned and headed for his cottage. Effie didn't move, not until she heard his door slam behind him.

NINE

"What are you doing here?" Parker's secretary glanced at the clock on the wall. "It's nearly five."

"And how are you, Anne?" He grinned as he walked past her into his office. "I thought I'd stop by and see how things are going."

Anne followed him to his doorway. He picked up his mail, then glanced at her. "Well?"

She shrugged. "We're surviving."

He knew what that meant. "Ben having problems?"

"The usual."

"Anything major?"

"Not really."

He studied Anne's face. Once he would have trusted her to tell him the truth. Since his stress attack, she'd been more protective.

"Honest," she insisted, smiling nervously.

"I want you to know, I am working on the problem."

"You're supposed to be on a vacation—relaxing—not working on any problems."

"I *am* relaxing," he insisted, though considering his

physical condition only an hour earlier, relaxing didn't seem the right term. Even now, he felt as tense as a caged tiger. Leaving Effie had taken him away from temptation, but hadn't lessened his desire to make love with her. "I'm also doing some serious thinking."

"About selling the business?"

"About a lot of things." Anne was one of a handful of his employees who knew about the Austin-Hill offer. Considering how many years she'd been with the store, and that after his father's death she'd practically taught him the ins and outs of the administrative side of running a retail business, he'd felt he needed to tell her he was considering the offer. He'd also wanted her input. She'd been no help, though. Anne had told him the decision was his and he had to do what was best for him.

Problem was, he didn't know what was best for him. To hold on to a legacy or to sell? To make love with Effie or stay far, far away from her?

That he was still pondering the question disturbed him. He hadn't let a woman bother him this much since Bernadette. For the last few years, making love or not making love had been simply a question of physical release, no emotions involved.

"You all right?" Anne asked, concern showing in her eyes.

He shrugged, denying the tension tearing at his insides. "I'm fine."

"Gene Hill did call today. I told him you were out of town."

"Good." Gene was pushing for a decision on the deal. Parker wasn't ready to make it.

Anne glanced back at the clock on the wall of her office. "Are you going to be needing me?"

"No." He wasn't sure what he was going to do or how long he was going to stay, but he didn't need a secretary. What he needed was a shrink. Maybe a psychiatrist could give him some answers.

Only he knew that wasn't true. Psychiatrists didn't give answers, merely made their patients look into themselves for answers. "Which I don't have."

"What?" Anne had started to turn away, but at the sound of his voice, she stopped and looked back.

"Nothing," he assured her. "Just mumbling to myself."

He'd done that the whole thirty-five miles from his cottage to the store. Mumbled, cursed himself, and questioned his sanity. "Go," he said, waving her on with a hand. "Shut off your computer, grab your purse, and get out of here."

"If you need me . . ." Anne hesitated, clearly unsure.

"I don't need you." He smiled reassuringly. "Actually, I doubt if I'll stay very long myself. I just wanted to go through my mail, maybe give my mother a call and see how she's doing."

"You're going back to the lake tonight, then?"

Parker was silent for a long moment.

"I'm not sure."

Effie wasn't sure when Parker had left his cottage and the lake. It was after five when she'd gone out to dump a load of garbage and saw his car was gone. He'd taken off. It was just as well, yet it reminded her too much of her father's pattern of behavior. Actually, it seemed like all of the men she knew took off. Whenever she'd dated someone she liked, something would come up and they'd be gone. Kent had certainly been no exception. Funny, once she'd convinced him she couldn't put on her clown outfit or makeup and wouldn't be dropping by his coffee shop to entertain his patrons—for free—he stopped calling her.

And now Parker . . .

No, she couldn't say Parker was like her father or the men she'd dated. He never had been and never would be. With Parker she felt a magic she couldn't explain. Being around him was like going to a circus. He made her all tingly inside, made her anxious, and made her laugh. She never knew what to expect, each moment exciting and a little scary. He brought the tears and he brought the smiles, and always when he left, he took the magic with him. She hadn't realized that so clearly until last Friday when he'd brought it back.

"And he'll never be yours," she said aloud, needing to remind herself. No more than she would ever be a circus clown.

She was surprised she'd thought of that. The idea of joining the circus hadn't crossed her mind in ages. For three years in a row, while she was still in college, she'd applied to the Clown College in Venice, Florida, hoping to become a Ringling Brothers and Barnum & Bailey Circus clown. For three years she'd been turned down. It didn't help to know that more than five thousand people applied each year and only thirty were chosen to attend the ten-week course. She hadn't been one of those thirty, and finally she'd given up and gone to a two-week clown camp. One of the best around. Lou Jacobs had been her instructor.

But now she wasn't even a clown anymore.

The sun set just before ten o'clock, and in the semi-darkness, Effie waded out into Gun Lake. The water lapped around her legs, cooling her body and soothing her thoughts. She'd accomplished a great deal in the hours since Parker had left. Staying busy had kept her from thinking. Only now, she needed to let weary muscles rest.

She had to walk out a long way before the water reached her waist. Only then did she sink to her shoulders, wetting her tank top. She hadn't bothered to put on a swimsuit. She'd barely remembered to take off her watch.

The water was pleasantly warm, and using long, easy strokes, Effie swam away from the shoreline and her grandparents' wooden dock. The world around her seemed unreal, lights from the houses and cottages along the shoreline beacons in the darkness. Distant voices and music blended with the croaking of frogs and singing of crickets. A few boats were still out on the water, bobbing red and green lights illuminating their presence. Otherwise, she was alone.

Mopsy gave an excited bark from the shoreline, and Effie rolled over onto her back and began lazily swimming back to shore. Mopsy always got worried when she went too far out. Mopsy definitely was not a water dog.

Only when her bottom hit sand did Effie stand. Wet curls clung to her face and she shook her head, flinging the excess water into the night. A brush of her hand removed any sand stuck to the back of her shorts and she twisted the water out of her top. Her clothing clinging to her body, she walked out of the lake and onto the grass.

Mopsy was nowhere in sight.

Parker absently stroked the silky hair of Mopsy's coat, his gaze locked on Effie. Above, clouds mingled with stars, the moon darting in and out. At the moment it was out and providing him with a very clear view of

Effie. The way her wet clothes clung to her body, she might as well have been wearing nothing. All his self-promises to stay relaxed were forgotten.

She called out Mopsy's name, a worried tone to her voice.

He answered. "Over here. I've got her."

Effie turned, facing him, and he stepped away from the shadows of his back door. Mopsy wiggled in his arms, and he let the dog down. She trotted toward Effie, but Effie continued looking at him. "How long have you been there?"

"Not long."

"I didn't know you'd returned."

Her glance traveled to his driveway. He'd parked on the far side, and from where she was standing, he doubted she could see his car. "I got here around nine."

"I guess I didn't expect you to come back."

"I wasn't sure I should."

He walked toward her slowly, drawn to her like metal to a magnet. He wasn't sure what he was doing. He had no plan, only a need.

Bad timing or not, he wanted to be with her, wanted to touch her. To hold her.

He wanted to make love with her.

"Parker?" Her voice held a note of panic, and she glanced at the water behind her, then at her back door. He grinned. He had her trapped between twenty-six hundred acres of water and a cottage with a bed. He hoped she chose the bed.

He stopped a few feet from her, giving her space. "How was your swim?"

"Good." She shivered.

"You're getting cold."

"No . . . I mean, yes." Again, she glanced toward her back door. "I'd better be going in."

"Good idea."

She started for the door, sidestepping up the grassy slope, always watching him. "Well, good night, Parker. See you tomorrow, I suppose."

"I'm sure you will." He followed her, keeping his distance. Mopsy trotted over to him, sniffing at his pants and leather shoes. Once again, he scooped her up. "Actually, I was hoping you'd invite me in tonight."

Effie stopped at her screen door, her hand on the knob. Between the moonlight and the lights she'd left on inside, he could see the expression on her face. Desire warred with a need for flight. He understood the battle; he'd been fighting it all afternoon.

"Are you sure that would be a good idea?" she asked.

He stepped closer. "Perhaps not, but I'd like to spend some time with you."

She shook her head, droplets of water scattering through the air, but she didn't say no. The way she was looking at him, he knew she didn't want to say no. With his free hand, he touched her face, his fingertips trailing a path from her cheek to her jaw. She didn't pull back, and he let his fingers slide down the side of her neck to her shoulder. He could feel her pulse. It was as wild as his.

For a moment the scooped neck of her tank top stopped the downward path of his hand, and his gaze dropped to the swell of her breasts. She'd changed. The cranberry-colored top had no spots of chocolate to lick; nevertheless, her nipples were erect nubs awaiting his touch. He accepted their invitation. Teasingly, he traced a circle around one with a finger and heard her suck in a breath.

Her eyes spoke without words, their color lost to the night. Pools of black emeralds that held the key to her soul. Eyes filled with questions he wasn't sure he could answer.

Parker knew only one thing. "I want to make love with you."

Through his fingertips, he could feel the rapid beat of her heart and the quick rise and fall of her breath. She moved her mouth, as if to speak, but no words came out. The tip of her tongue moistened her lips, and she tried again. "I never thought—"

She didn't finish, but he understood. "I didn't either, but ever since I saw you Friday morning—"

It was his turn not to finish. Gently, he moved her aside and reached for the doorknob.

Effie wasn't sure how Parker got her into the cottage, but the next thing she knew, he was closing the door and snapping off the light. He put Mopsy down, and Effie watched the dog trot off to the kitchen. Foolishly, she wanted to call her back, as if something weighing twelve pounds could protect her from the man standing in front of her.

A hand touched her shoulder, and she gasped, looking back up at Parker.

"I'm not going to attack you," he said softly.

She knew that, yet she couldn't stop the shaking in her legs or the turmoil in her stomach. Once she'd had daydreams of this moment, and she'd thought she would know exactly what to say and do. Now she could only stare up at the shadowy outline of his face and marvel at the chiseled perfection of his features.

He brushed a wet, dangling curl back from her face and smiled tenderly. "You look as scared as you did that night when you were sixteen, and I kissed you."

"I'm not scared," she said. "Not of you."

What frightened her was the enormity of the feelings he aroused within her. She'd made love before,
with two men she'd thought she truly cared for. But
when they'd touched her, she hadn't been shaken to the
core, as she was with Parker. When they'd kissed her,
she hadn't felt her universe go off-kilter, as it did every
time Parker kissed her. She was afraid to find out what
making love with him would do to her. Making love
with Parker might turn into a lot more than an act of
sex. "Making love" might become "falling in love."

She stepped back, again shaking her head. "This
isn't going to work."

He caught her by the shoulders, stopping her retreat. "I'm not asking for a lifetime commitment."

That was the problem.

A little pressure applied behind her shoulders, and
he had her stepping forward again. She put her hands
between them, keeping her body from touching his.
"I'm going to get you wet."

He barely glanced down at his pale blue cotton dress
shirt and gray slacks. "I don't care."

"What about Bernadette?"

"What about her?"

"She . . . You—"

"There is no she and I," he said succinctly. "Hasn't
been for years."

"But . . ."

Effie couldn't say anything more. Parker's mouth
covering hers swallowed any further protests, and she
found reason giving way to sensations. The heat of desire rushed through her like a wildfire. A flick of his
tongue teased the flames, and her body responded.
Melting against him, she parted her lips, welcoming the
penetration. Her knees buckled, his strength alone holding her on her feet, his magic weaving its spell over her.

Sending him away was no longer an option; the word *no* had disappeared from her vocabulary. The question of Bernadette faded to oblivion, and Effie shivered, tremors of excitement cascading through her.

"You're cold," he said, drawing back to look at her. "We need to get you out of these wet clothes."

"I'm—I'm okay." She stammered over the words, knowing she was anything but okay.

"How about a hot shower?"

The way he said it, she knew she wouldn't be showering alone. The idea of bathing with him, of seeing him naked—being naked with him—sent another shiver through her body, yet she didn't stop him when he guided her toward the bathroom.

He shut the door behind them and turned on the water, testing it for temperature before turning to face her. Wide-eyed, she watched his every gesture. She hadn't moved from the spot where he'd released his hold on her, not that he'd really released his hold. She was his, if only for the night. His gaze held her captive, his smile drawing her to him. Willingly, she lifted her arms, and he removed her tank top.

His smile became lusty as his gaze raked down her body. She looked down herself, knowing her breasts were swollen from his touch, her nipples hard and rigid. She watched him reach out, one large, masculine hand covering each breast, encompassing her fullness. The rough texture of his skin awakened new sensations within her, sending vibrations of need through her body and tightening the muscles of her loins. One thing alone, she knew, would ease that tension. A coming together, a melding of body and soul.

"I don't know if we're going to get into that shower," he said huskily, his breathing ragged.

"I don't need a shower to warm me." She unbuttoned his shirt and it fell on the linoleum, next to hers.

Effie slipped off her wet shorts and panties while Parker took off his shoes. He started to unbuckle his belt, but she took over, pulling down the zipper. Only when he raked his fingers through her hair did she look up. His smile was all-consuming, the fire in his eyes blazing its way to her heart.

He tipped her head back and kissed her. Firmly. Passionately. His slacks dropped to the floor, and he brought her hips against his, only a single layer of cotton separating their bodies. The heat and the hardness of his arousal pressed against her belly, triggering a moistness within her. She hooked her fingers under the elastic waistband of his briefs and pulled downward.

"Easy," he warned, helping her. His hand slid between their hips, his fingertips brushing over the triangle of hair between her legs. His briefs dropped to the floor, but his hand stayed where it was.

Parker teased her lips with his, but it was the foray of his fingers that held her attention. A small gasp escaped her throat as he found her most sensitive spot and rubbed the pad of a finger over it. He repeated the motion, and the sound turned into a moan of ecstasy. The thrust of his tongue, deep into her mouth, echoed another thrusting. Her control was in danger of dissolving, her legs too weak to hold her.

"Parker," she pleaded, afraid she would crumple to the floor.

"Do you want me?" he asked.

"Yes." Completely. Senselessly.

"Inside of you?"

"Yes." Her answer was a groan, her body begging for relief.

He eased her down onto the fluffy bath mat she'd

bought for her grandmother only the year before, its fibers cushioning her from the hardness of the linoleum floor. Behind him, the shower continued to run, turning the air steamy. Nothing seemed real, the room a hazy haven of warm mist. Yet everything was real.

Parker knelt over her and kissed her, first on the mouth, then on her breasts, sucking at each nipple. She raked her fingers through his hair, holding him to her. She wanted to capture every sensation, never forget the electricity each lick of his tongue generated. Even her toes tingled, and when he dipped his tongue into her naval, she couldn't stop a shudder.

"Naval attack," she joked, needing a relief from the tension.

He lifted his head, his eyes dark with passion. "And now we're going for a deep dive."

The moment he touched her between her legs, she understood. Nevertheless, she wasn't prepared for the touch of his tongue, and she closed her eyes at the exquisite sensation.

Insanity was only a breath away. She wanted him to stop . . . and she wanted him never to stop. He moved over her, rubbing his hips against hers, teasing her with his hardness. The ache within her screamed for satisfaction, pleasure mingling with torture. She wanted him inside of her, filling her.

Grabbing his shoulders, she gasped her plea. "Parker, please—"

He sat back on his haunches, surprising her. She watched him lean over and turn off the shower, the spattering water reduced to a trickle, then nothing. Reaching for his slacks, he began digging in one pocket.

"When I decided to come back," he explained, pulling out a small box and extracting a foil packet, "I knew this was how we'd end up." His gaze snapped back to her face. "At least, this is what I hoped would happen, so I stopped at the store on my way back."

"Meaning you don't always have those in your pocket?"

He shook his head, fumbling with the foil, and she knew he was telling the truth. His hand was shaking, and she realized he was as nervous as she was. Reaching out, she took the packet and carefully opened it.

She held it toward him, but he again shook his head. "Put it on me."

Effie glanced down at his hips. His readiness was evident, and she knew he wasn't a man who would ever be embarrassed in the locker room. Without realizing she was doing it, she licked her lips, then looked up at his face. He was smiling.

Taking her hands in his, he helped her.

Parker felt her fingers tremble. He was trembling inside. He hadn't been this excited since he'd been in his teens. Then he'd been with Bernadette, and barely in control. His first time with her, he'd finished before she'd even begun. With Effie, he wanted everything to be perfect. He wanted to make her happy, to bring her pleasure. Except, the way she made him feel, he wasn't sure he would last.

Gazing down at her face, he marveled at her natural beauty. Wet, her hair was a deep auburn and created a rich contrast to the white rug. Her skin was translucent and flushed, her freckles a comedic accent across the bridge of her nose and over her cheeks. He traced their pattern with one finger, then leaned close to kiss her. Thick lashes, a shade lighter than her hair, fluttered closed, then rose to reveal a fire in a bed of emeralds.

That he'd ignited that fire excited him. He wanted to warm himself in her glow, to be consumed by her heat. He nibbled at her earlobes, first one, then the other, catching the small golden studs she wore. His tongue darting into her ear made her wiggle her thighs pressing against his legs, reminding him of exactly where he was poised. Rubbing against her, he teased her, even as he teased himself, and heard the soft sound that escaped from deep within her throat. A kiss on her lips sealed the bond, her response conveying her willingness even as her body was stating her readiness.

Every mile of his drive away from her that afternoon had been merely a temporary escape from the inevitable. He should have known he couldn't stay away. The pull had been there from the beginning, from Friday morning, when he first saw her. Perhaps from thirteen years ago, when he'd realized she was more than a child . . . more than the little sister. Back then, he'd fled to New York and blocked her from his thoughts. No longer could he ignore what he felt.

What he wanted.

He parted her legs, pressing gently at first, unwilling to hurt her even though the one thing he wanted most was to thrust himself deep into her silky treasure. With his hands, he touched and caressed her, seeking ways to give her pleasure, her ragged breathing his guide. Inside of her, he felt her response. Swelling around him, she moved her hips. He gauged his rhythm to match hers, each thrust stronger and deeper until he knew she was teetering on the edge.

He was teetering on the edge. Hold on, he told himself, praying he could.

"Hold on," he gasped as spasms took her beyond the edge, and she held on, her fingernails digging deep into his back and her legs clamped tight against his.

She held him to her, deep inside of her, her moans of pleasure exciting him beyond sanity. Releasing all constraints, he surged into her, quickening the rhythm.

His heart pounded wildly and his lungs ached for air, but not even the possibility of a heart attack would have slowed his thrusts. Fears were forgotten, self-doubts put aside. For the moment he knew why he existed and what he wanted. Nothing could have been clearer.

His release came with a sudden rush, rocketing through him. He gasped and cried out, letting it take him. Head thrown back, his eyes closed, he savored every marvelous sensation.

Spent, he took in a deep breath. He wanted to crow. He wanted to beat his fists against his chest and yell like Tarzan. He wanted to—

He looked down at Effie. Her eyes were wide with wonder, her lips parted, and he knew exactly what he wanted to do. Bending close, he kissed her.

TEN

They did take a shower, but by the time they were finished, Parker's kisses had Effie shivering with excitement and as out of control as before. The boxes she'd piled on her bed were tossed onto the floor with no concern for what was in them. Effie couldn't believe how uninhibited she'd become. All she wanted was to be held by Parker, kissed by him . . . made love to.

Mopsy certainly couldn't understand what was going on. The first time she jumped on the bed, Parker gently set her back on the floor. The second time, Effie firmly ordered her off. And when Mopsy barked her displeasure with the new sleeping arrangements, Parker scooted her out of the bedroom and closed the door.

Twenty minutes later they let her back in.

Jealously, Mopsy pushed her way between them, snuggling close to Effie. Parker stroked the dog's head, chuckling. "I think we may have a problem."

"She doesn't share well."

"I don't blame her."

Effie rubbed a foot over Parker's bare leg. That he was lying in her bed, had made love to her—twice—was still beyond her comprehension. "I think I'm dreaming."

Reaching over Mopsy, Parker caressed her cheek. "We're having the same dream."

"It's so funny. I feel like I've known you a lifetime, yet I don't know you at all." She lowered her gaze, the truth hitting her. "I've just made love with a stranger."

He turned her head so she was looking at him. "I've been called strange, but we're certainly not strangers. Effie, you probably know me as well as anyone does."

"I didn't know you'd gone to New York, that you'd tried to write a book. Not until this weekend. I've always thought of you as being ultraconservative. A staid and stolid businessman. Someone who—" She couldn't say it. "Someone who wouldn't—"

He arched his eyebrows. "Do anything my parents didn't have planned for me?"

"When I knew you, that's how it was. Oh, you talked about wanting to be a writer, but I always thought it was just talk, especially when your mother told me you'd gone back to college and that you weren't coming to the lake because you were busy with the business."

"But now you know different."

"Yes, but—" Saying what she felt was not easy. "You did end up as the head of Morgan's Department Stores. Maybe it took the death of your father, but ultimately you've done exactly what they wanted. Not only that, you're so involved with those stores, it's killing you, just as it killed your father."

"If I let it."

"Do you really think you can change?" She had her doubts. "Can you turn your back on that business as easily as you did on your great American novel?"

He arched back, a slight frown indicating his displeasure with her words. "And what do you think?"

"I think the sophisticated man I see on the television ads has taken over the writer. I think coming back to the lake has made you remember some of the feelings you had when you were twenty, but I don't think you can really turn away from the business. Consider this, Parker. Friday you went back to the store. Sunday you took Bern there. This evening—"

"This evening I needed some time away from you, time to think."

She hesitated, then shook her head. "I never should have let you in this cottage."

"Are you now sorry that we made love?"

She closed her eyes, wishing she could lie. Her no was barely audible.

"Then what?"

"This is going to hurt too much."

Even with her eyes closed, she felt his gaze sweep over her body. "I hurt you?"

"I mean later." She looked at him again, needing him to understand. "Parker, maybe you wanted me that night thirteen years ago, and maybe you wanted me tonight, but I'm not someone you're going to be interested in long term."

"Why not?" Again, his gaze raked over her. "You're attractive, interesting . . . fun to be around."

"Attractive, maybe, but not beautiful. Not stunning or sexy. Not like Bern. And I don't have"—she hesitated, then threw out the word she'd learned to hate—"class."

"Forget that 'class' business. I thought that was what I wanted. Now I realize the one looking for a 'woman with class' was my mother, not me." He chuckled softly. "I talked to Mom tonight. I told her I'd run into you and Bern, and that I might be hiring Bern to be my general manager. She mentioned that she'd always felt Bernadette had class."

"And?" It was Ruth Morgan's opinion of her that Effie wanted to hear.

"And . . ." He took his time, combining his words with a gentle caressing of her face. "My mother said that you'd always worried her."

"I worried *her*?" His mother had never appeared worried. Aloof, yes. Snobbish, yes. But worried? "Why?"

"You were 'spirited,' she said." He smiled. "I think my parents always felt they could mold Bernadette, but you—" He shook his head. "My father used to say you bounced rather than walked. He called you a free spirit. If you sensed disapproval from them, it was because they were afraid of you."

"You're kidding." It wasn't something she would have guessed. "I can't believe they were worried about me."

"Clowns can be scary." He tweaked her nose. "And they were right. You did talk me into going to New York."

"You said I didn't talk you into that. Besides, you did all the talking that night," she reminded him. "I just listened."

"And said, 'If that's what you want to do, do it.' I'm not trying to lay any guilt on you, I'm just saying they were right. And it wasn't just that night. Over those three summers that I knew you, through your jokes and your kidding, you made me see what a robot I'd become. There I was, practically a grown man, being led around by my parents like a little boy. I've felt guilty as hell about not being there for my father, but on the other hand, one thing I've learned since having this attack of mine, what killed my father was a weakness he was born with. It was a time bomb, just waiting to kill him. I also know, if I hadn't gone to New York, I would have always wondered if I could have made it. That day, when I thought I was dying, one of the thoughts running through my head was, at least I'd given the writing a shot."

"And you could do it again. Two years isn't enough time to know if you're good or not. Give it another shot."

He shrugged. "Maybe. I don't know. The desire's not as strong. I have a feeling the act of rebelling, of doing something exactly opposite of what my parents wanted, was more important than writing a book. I think I'm more of a realist now. Or at least, I was until one shrimp of a redhead started twisting me in knots so I can't think straight." Balancing himself over Mopsy, he kissed her.

With a snort, Mopsy scooted out from between them and jumped off the bed. She went over to a corner and lay down, her chin on her paws, her long, silky hair touching the carpeting, and her dark button eyes focused on them.

"I think she's upset," Parker said. "Is she always like this when you have a man in bed?"

"No."

He looked back at Effie. She'd answered too easily for his comfort. He didn't want to think of Effie with other men. Sinking back on the bed, he stared at her ceiling. "You're right. We don't know each other very well. People change in thirteen years. Grow up." He chanced a glance at her. "Have there been many? Men, I mean."

"No."

She answered softly, and he looked away, closing his

eyes. "I shouldn't have even asked. It's none of my business."

"I don't mind telling you." She laughed, forcing his attention back to her. She was on her side now, looking right at him. "Actually, there's not much to tell. I don't have very good luck with men. It's my fault. I have this habit of picking guys who either aren't ready to commit or can't express their emotions."

"That's probably how women describe me." Not that he was proud of the label. "There was one woman I met in New York who I really liked, but after Dad died, that sort of fell apart. Everything sort of fell apart after his death. Women, I've discovered, don't hang around long when you only ask them out once every few weeks."

"We do tend to get cranky about that, feel neglected."

"I never meant to neglect any of them. I've just been busy. First, getting everything in order after my father died, then learning the business. After that came the idea of opening stores in Kalamazoo and Lansing. Up until this past May, it wasn't unusual for me to be in the office until ten or eleven every night, weekends included."

"A true workaholic. No wonder your body yelled for help."

"According to my doctor, I'd become obsessive over my work. Now I have to learn to play. Have to get a hobby."

"To be taken once a day. *A life.*" Effie mimicked in tone and gestures a doctor writing a prescription. "Patient will play some golf. Go fishing. Make love."

Parker grinned. "So far, I like the 'make love' part best. The golf has been so-so, and the fishing sucks. I was out three hours this morning. Me, the gulls, and the mosquitoes. I don't know where the fish were. Certainly not on the end of my line."

"Grandpa always said you have to know where to fish this lake."

"I remember the time he took us out." Parker cuddled Effie closer. "That was fun."

"You caught a lot of fish that day. Certainly more than I did." She tweated at the hairs on his chest. "But you cheated."

"How's that?"

"You kept smiling at me, and I couldn't think straight."

"Excuses, excuses. I suppose you're also going to blame me for the time you fell off the horse when we went riding."

"Who else?"

"Maybe the person who decided to stand on the saddle. Not *in* the saddle, but *on* it."

"Hey, they do it all the time in the circus, and I was doing fine until you turned around and looked at me."

"You are a nut, you know." He kissed her just below the red lock of hair touching the middle of her forehead, his thoughts jumping back to the time he'd taken her horseback riding. Her father was supposed to take her that day. He'd been at the lake for one of his rare visits. Effie had been so excited about going riding with her father, she'd come bouncing out of the cottage with the news. An hour later she'd come back out with her shoulders slumped and the sparkle gone from her eyes. Her father had gotten a call and had changed his plans. He was leaving sooner than expected. There would be no horseback ride.

Parker had felt so sorry for her, he'd taken her himself.

"You were my Prince Charming that day," she said.

"I remember you swinging off your horse and bending over me. You looked so worried." She grinned. "I wanted you to kiss me, but, of course, you didn't."

"I *was* worried," he said. "One minute you were standing on the back of that horse, the next you were crumpled on the ground. You scared me to death. All I could think was you'd broken your neck. Or your back. Or a leg, at best."

"But I didn't."

"No, you didn't." She hadn't even cried. He'd helped her up, and she'd gotten back on her horse and had finished the ride as if nothing had happened. He'd known she was embarrassed, and he'd promised to take her again. He never did.

"I don't blame you for never taking me again," she said, as if reading his mind. "Who wants to take a girl riding who can't even stay on a horse?"

"You ride very well, and you know it." He'd been impressed. "What about tomorrow?"

Her eyebrows lifted. "Tomorrow?"

"Want to go riding? I know Flying Horseshoe is still open. I'm willing to give it another try if you are. That is, if you promise not to do any stunts."

"You mean I'd have to sit in the saddle, feet in the stirrups and hands on the reins?"

"Yep."

"Bern and I are supposed to work on this place tomorrow."

"You're assuming Bern makes it before dinnertime."

"She'd better."

"Okay, I'll make you a deal. I'll help you with the cleanup here, we take an hour, hour and a half to ride, and everyone's happy."

"You really feel that guilty about not taking me again?"

"Is it a date or not?"

She smiled. "It's a date."

Her smile was enticing, and once again, he leaned over her. "Is it too late for Prince Charming to claim that kiss?"

"It's never too late." Effie slipped her arms around his neck and pulled him closer.

Waking up, Effie remembered many summer mornings throughout her childhood when the air had had the same fresh smell, the sun flooding through the window had had the same bright warmth, and the sounds outside had included children laughing. What was different this morning was the body next to hers.

Even when Bernadette was eighteen, she'd never taken up so much space in the bed, and she'd never made deep grumbly sounds, or smelled so alluringly masculine. Parker's dark lashes rested on his cheeks, his breathing even. Effie treasured his sleep. Daylight often destroyed the illusions of night, and she didn't want this dream to end, not yet.

He was her Prince Charming, her knight in shining armor. He was also a man, virile and exciting. He'd awakened in her new sensations, triggered a lust she'd never known she possessed. Simply looking at him, at the breadth of his brow, straight line of his nose, and solid cut of his jaw stirred a need she'd thought they'd sated.

She wanted to touch him, run her fingers over the dark stubble of beard on his chin. She wanted him to hold her close again, crushing her beneath his weight, yet not crushing her. To hear his cry of satisfaction and know she'd caused it.

From near her feet, she felt a movement. Glancing

that way, she saw Mopsy. She didn't know when the dog had come back up on the bed, but from the way Mopsy was looking at her, Effie knew what was next. "Need to go out?" she whispered, and Mopsy wagged her tail.

Effie slid out from beneath the covers as carefully as she could, not wanting to disturb Parker. She grabbed an oversized T-shirt from the duffel bag she'd brought up from Kalamazoo and slipped it on, then let Mopsy out. While her dog found the right patch of grass, Effie took care of her own needs.

Standing in front of the vanity mirror, she smiled. Her cheeks had a ruddy glow. Whisker burn, undoubtedly, but she preferred to think of it as the glow of happiness. "I made love with Parker Morgan."

Hearing the words aloud sent a shiver through her body, and she glanced down at the rug where they'd done it the first time. The day she'd picked that rug out for her grandmother, if anyone had told her she would make love with Parker on it, she would have said they were crazy. Absolutely crazy.

"You're the one who's gone crazy," she muttered to herself, and went back to brushing her teeth.

Insanity, she decided, was great. A lack of sleep didn't bother her. She'd never felt so energized, and once she was certain she didn't need to worry about "morning breath," and her hair was as tamed as she could manage after all the times Parker had run his fingers through it, she began picking up.

Parker's shirt was damp from lying on top of her wet tank top, but his slacks and briefs were dry. She carried them to her bedroom, tiptoeing in so she wouldn't wake him, and laid them across the bottom of the bed. The wet clothing, she dropped into her grandmother's old washing machine. In an hour, his shirt would be clean and dry.

Surprised that Mopsy wasn't at the door begging to come in, Effie went looking for her. She found her at the neighbors', playing with two children, and a quick performance was inevitable. Mopsy did her routine, Effie played the fool, and the children laughed. It wasn't until she started back to the cottage, Mopsy in her arms, that Effie saw Parker watching her through the screen door. "Morning, sleepyhead," she called as she neared.

"You should have woken me." He held the door open for her.

"I thought you might like to sleep in." He'd slipped on his slacks, but was bare-chested. Effie set Mopsy down, then reached out and toyed with a lock of dark hair on Parker's chest. "I'm washing your shirt. It was wet."

He caught her hand between his, bringing her fingers to his mouth. "I ran into a mermaid last night."

"Hmm." She faked a concerned look. "The doctors are right, you have been working too hard. You're now seeing mermaids?"

Grinning, he kissed her fingertips. "I don't know about working too hard, but *something* was hard last night."

His implication was clear, and immediately the muscles between her legs tightened, her voice turning gravelly. "Very hard."

"It's still hard."

A hug brought her hips against his, and she knew he was right. Any fears she'd had of his interest waning disappeared. The look in his eyes said the chemistry was still there, waiting to be mixed.

"What's for breakfast?" he asked softly.

"What would you like?"

His smile gave his answer, and he led her back to the bedroom.

Effie cracked another egg into the bowl and glanced at the clock on the kitchen wall. Making breakfast at noon was crazy. Making love all night and morning was crazy. She loved it. " 'I could fall in love with you,' " she sang.

"In love," she repeated, knowing it was safe to say the words aloud. Parker had gone to his place to make coffee. "Real coffee," he'd stated when she'd offered him instant.

"I, Effie Leigh Sanders, am in love with Parker Morgan." The words scared and soothed her. Everything had happened so quickly, yet it had taken a lifetime to happen. Providence *was* at work. It simply wasn't working for Bernadette.

"Serves you right for not coming Friday," Effie muttered. "If you'd been here then. Here yesterday. Here—"

She cut off her monologue. Bernadette Sanders *was* here. The purr of the Acura's engine was unmistakable. Stepping closer to the window, Effie looked toward the drive and saw her sister slide out of her car.

Bernadette was stylishly dressed, as always. Her beige-and-brown slacks outfit looked chic, not a strand of her hair was out of place, and her makeup was picture-perfect. She was beauty, sophistication, and class, all rolled into one.

But I got him, shot through Effie's head.

As soon as she thought it, she grimaced. She didn't want to be in competition with her sister. Didn't want to take something from Bern.

Bernadette glanced toward Parker's place, and the acids of guilt poured into Effie's stomach. How did you tell your sister you'd made love with her former boyfriend? "Oh, by the way, last night Parker and I made whoopee into the wee hours. Hope you don't mind."

Bernadette would mind.

"Why did I do it?" Effie murmured, yet she knew why. She'd wanted to.

But for what reason?

Love? Did she really love him? Or was it simply to prove to herself that she could win his interest? That she could take him away from Bernadette?

The thought made her sick, and the ache in her joints, puffiness of her lips, and tenderness of her nipples were no longer wonderful sensations. She was a dirty, rotten sister. That's what she was.

The screen door slammed shut, and Effie cringed. Smiling, Bernadette came into the kitchen. "Wow, you've done a lot."

"Not all that much." Certainly not as much as she could have accomplished if she hadn't spent the morning making love with Parker.

"Sorry I've had to be gone so much." Bern casually strolled across the room to look out the kitchen window that faced Parker's place. "I've really shirked my duties."

"Well, you're here now." Effie hoped Parker didn't come back for a few minutes. Not until she had a chance to talk to Bern. "I, ah . . . That is—"

"Is he home?" Bern interrupted.

"Parker? Yes. But he's . . . That is, he and I—We—"

Bern faced her. "I'm going over to talk to him. You were right, you know. Fate did bring us together. Parker changed my life once. Looks like he's going to do it again."

Effie hoped she understood. "You're going to take the job?"

"He told you about it?" Bern looked surprised, then smiled and nodded. "I think so. Not that I'm going to tell him that right away. You know how men like women who are hard to get." Her grin expanded. "This woman is going to be very hard to get, but don't be surprised if I spend the night at his place."

An image of Parker with Bernadette flashed through Effie's mind, and she went cold inside. Unable to say anything, she watched Bernadette leave. Watched and listened. The screen door banged closed, and Bern left humming. Through the open window, Effie heard her sister's faint knock on Parker's door, followed by her soft, sexy, "Hello there. Anybody home?"

Bernadette returned a half hour later. Effie watched her pick up her purse from the table and check her reflection in a hand mirror before turning toward her. Bern's smile was triumphant. "I think things are going to work out just fine. We're going to Grand Rapids."

Effie knew before she even asked. "When?"

"As soon as I touch up my lipstick. Oh, and Parker said to tell you, he's sorry, but the horseback ride he was going to take you on will have to be postponed."

"He's canceling our date to take you to Grand Rapids?" She knew he was the one she should be angry with, but Bernadette's smile irked Effie. She stepped up to her sister, silently cursing the genetic makeup that made her a good six inches shorter.

"He's going to give me another tour of the stores." Bern pulled a lipstick from her purse. "I'm going to get that pitch I can't refuse. A little sweet talk."

The pain cutting through Effie was too great to hold inside. She wanted to wail or to scream. To pummel Bern with her fists. What she did was lash out verbally.

"And what about this place?" Effie waved a hand to encompass the entire cottage. "While you're waltzing off to Grand Rapids with Mr. Parker Morgan, who's going to get things ready for that yard sale Friday? So far the only one doing any work around here has been me. You couldn't come Friday. You had to be gone Monday. Now you're going to be gone today."

Bernadette put down her lipstick. "I'll help you tomorrow. After all, you weren't planning on being here anyway. You and Parker were going riding. Why don't you still go riding?"

"Maybe I don't want to go riding."

Bern lifted her eyebrows. "Then don't. Didn't Parker help you yesterday?"

"Yes, Parker helped me yesterday." And made love with her. And now he was taking off with Bernadette.

"As far as I can see, the two of you got a lot accomplished."

Effie didn't want to talk about Parker and what they'd accomplished. She didn't want to think about him. "I need *your* help. We need to figure out which of Grandma and Grandpa's things we want to keep, what we want to sell, and what we want to toss. We only have two weeks in all to get this place ready. At least, *I* only have two weeks. Unlike you, I can't walk away from my job. I have a partner who expects me to do my fair share."

"Fair share." Bern scoffed. "You sound just like you did when we were kids. 'Grandma, she didn't do her fair share.'"

"If I sound like a kid, it's—it's because you're acting like a kid, thinking only of yourself."

"And who else is going to think about me? Take care of me?" Bern dropped the lipstick back in her purse and snapped it shut. "That's one thing Dad taught me. Take care of yourself."

"And leave the packing to others." Effie glared at her. "I also learned a few things from Dad. I learned people let you down. Well, you want to go to Grand Rapids? Go! You want Parker? Fine! You can have him!"

"I want this job, that's what I want. What's the matter with you, anyway?" Bernadette frowned. "It's not like the world is going to come to an end if we don't get this place on the market in two weeks. We'll get it done."

"Nothing's the matter," Effie snapped, and knew that was a lie. Everything was the matter. She hadn't made love with Parker because she wanted to take him from her sister. She'd made love with him because she loved him.

And now he was going off with Bernadette, might spend the night with Bernadette.

"Go on. Get the job." She waved her hand toward the door and managed a smile. "Blame my behavior on PMS."

"I'll help tomorrow. I promise," Bern said, her tone softer. Stepping close, she hugged Effie. "Everything's going to be all right. I know this is hard on you. You and Grandma were so close. I miss her too."

Effie bit back tears and wished they were for her grandmother.

ELEVEN

The first thing Parker noticed as he drove down England Drive was that Effie's car was gone. Only Bern's sporty white Acura and their grandparents' Buick awaited their return. The absence of Effie's car bothered him, and Bernadette caught his concern. "Maybe she did decide to go riding."

"Maybe." He doubted it.

After he'd parked, Parker parted company with Bern. He had papers he'd picked up at his office that he wanted to read through later. He expected to find a note from Effie at his cottage. What she'd left was his shirt, neatly folded in a plastic bag hanging from his doorknob. It went on his kitchen table, along with the papers, and he headed for the Sanderses' cottage. Bern came out as he neared, a note in her hand. "She's gone."

"Gone?" The word sounded too final, and wasn't what he wanted to hear. What he wanted was to see Effie, to touch her. It had been five hours since he'd held her in his arms and made love with her.

He'd been thinking of her all the while he was with

Bern in Grand Rapids. They'd toured both stores this time, the Morgan's on Twenty-eighth Street and the one downtown. Bern's coy pretense of only casual interest didn't fool him. He knew she wanted the job he was offering, wanted it bad. He also knew she'd be good. Bernadette, unlike Ben, was firm, savvy, and decisive. His associates would respect her, and so would the sales reps.

He credited Bernadette's savvy for the speed with which she'd picked up on his interest in Effie. As they'd driven into Grand Rapids, and while they were touring the stores, he'd thought he was cloaking his questions about Effie in casual conversation. It had been a waste of time. On the drive back to the lake, Bernadette had confronted him. All he'd admitted was his attraction to Effie was growing. Bern's smile had said the rest. She understood.

Which was more than he could claim. He neither understood his attraction to Effie Sanders nor the emptiness within him that her absence was creating. All he knew was he wanted to see her, to be with her.

Bernadette handed him the note. "This was on the kitchen table, and her duffel bag and Mopsy's food and dishes are gone."

Parker read the short note at a glance.

Sorry for the blowup. I yell at you for leaving me with all the work, and now I'm taking off and leaving you. I can't explain, but I need to talk to Bubbles. I'll be back sometime Wednesday.

He looked back up at Bernadette. "Who's Bubbles?"

"A clown. He's like her mentor."

"He?" Parker didn't like the jealousy that grabbed his gut.

Bern smiled. "Don't worry. The man has got to be in his seventies. Has a wife. He's become like a father figure to her. I know she talks to him whenever she has a problem."

"Where's he live?"

"I'm not sure." Bern walked down to the edge of the water, her gaze directed toward the two small islands lying in East Gun Lake. "Somewhere around Three Rivers, I think. I wish I'd known about you two when I talked to her today. I wouldn't have said some of the things I said."

Her tone was casual, but Parker sensed trouble. "What did you say?"

Bern glanced at him, then back at the expanse of water in front of her. "She may think I'm still interested in you."

He said nothing, simply waited, and as he'd expected, Bernadette turned back toward him. Using a hand to shield her eyes from the glare of the sun, she finished her statement. "I may have given her the impression that we would be doing more than discussing business today . . . and tonight."

"You told her we'd be spending the night together?" He was beginning to understand why Effie had left.

Bern shrugged. "Suggested it. How was I to know your tastes in women had changed?"

The fist clenching his gut closed tighter. Parker could imagine Effie's reaction to Bernadette's "suggestion." From the beginning Effie had expected him to get back together with her sister. She hadn't expected him to be interested in her any more than he'd been prepared for the feelings he'd been experiencing these last few days.

Their relationship was too new. He needed to talk to her, to explain. Except, she was gone.

Gone to see a man who lived somewhere around Three Rivers. And after she talked to him? Parker stepped toward Bernadette. "Give me directions to her place in Kalamazoo."

Clown posters hung in the pane-glass windows of the small party shop on West Main, and clamorous laughter sounded the moment Effie opened the door. It stopped when the door closed. A mural with life-size clowns decorated one wall, ceramic and porcelain statues filled display cases, and a live green-and-red parrot sat on a perch near a clock shaped like a clown's face. The hands on the clock showed ten thirty-five, but Clowning Around was nearly empty. Only one customer browsed through the section of party invitations.

The parrot squawked a greeting, and Mopsy enthusiastically barked back. Tail wagging, she trotted past the tall brunette behind the checkout counter and went straight to the parrot, who jabbered excitedly. Effie proceeded at a slower rate, ignoring the noisy welcome that always occurred when dog and bird were reunited. She was more concerned by her business partner-and-friend's appearance.

Joan's nose was nearly as red as Effie's hair, her eyes watery, and the smile and sparkle that were always a part of her personality were missing. Effie frowned. "You look terrible, Joan."

"I godda code. Quied!" she yelled at the barking dog and jabbering bird, then looked back at Effie. "Whad are joo two doing here?"

"I came to get my extra makeup. I figured, as long as Bern and I are having that yard sale at the lake, I might as well try selling my clowning gear. All of it."

"Yer therious?" Joan frowned, then sneezed and grabbed a tissue from the box on the counter.

Effie nodded and waited for her to blow her nose. "I

spent the night with Bubbles and his wife. He said he's known others who have had similar experiences—just couldn't put on the face anymore, no matter how hard they tried. Of course, he thinks I should give myself more time before I make this decision, but I don't see why. I just can't do it. I know I'm letting you down, but—"

Joan shook her head. "Joo habbent let me down."

"Haven't I?" Effie could list the times. "How about all the parties Effie the Effervescent has been scheduled for in the last four months that you've had to do?"

"Joo've been habbing ah bad time. I under'tood."

"Well, I don't understand." Effie wished she did. "I don't know why I can't put on that outfit. Why I can't put on the makeup." Her gaze met Joan's. "Just the other day I went to see a sick child. I could let Mopsy perform, I could even do my part of the routine with her, but I couldn't actually do my clowning bit. And when Mandy asked me to entertain at her birthday party, it was like she was asking me to tear my insides out. The idea of becoming Effie the Effervescent again . . ." She shook her head. "I knew I couldn't do it. Joan, I used to think of myself as a giving person. Now all I do is take."

"Yer still ah gibbing person. Yer just habbing ah rough time."

Effie continued to shake her head. "I've become just like my father. All I think about is myself. I was too busy for my grandmother when she needed me. That little girl needs me, and all I can think of is myself. And then Monday night—"

She stopped. What she'd done Monday night was deplorable. Unforgivable. She'd made love with her sister's boyfriend. While Bern was away, Effie had played.

"Whad habbend Monday night?"

Effie had known Joan for six years. They'd gone through clown camp together, had worked parties together, and together had daydreamed of owning their own party store. Clowning Around was the result of those daydreams. They'd also gone through boyfriends together. Not that they'd shared men, but they had shared their ups and downs. More than once, when they were down and thrashing men royally, Effie had talked about Parker.

"Remember that guy I've told you about that my sister went with for three years, the one who put the make on me one night then took off, never to be seen again?"

"Da mystery man? Da one you won't tell be da name ub?"

Effie nodded. "Well, he's at the lake. And my sister thinks she can get something started with him again. Except, while she was gone, I got something started with him."

Joan's eyebrows did a quizzical lift.

Effie knew she understood. "I saw, I wanted, and I took. I knew I shouldn't, but I still did it. I am now truly like my father. I don't care about other people's feelings. As I told Bubbles, I don't think I deserve to be a clown."

"Joo tink too much. Wad joo need to do—"

Joan sneezed again, and Effie knew what she needed to do. As a half partner in the business, she had equal say in how it was run, who worked, and who didn't. She pointed at the door. "Go home. Go to bed. Get well."

"I can't. I godda be here to take care ub da customers."

"I'll stay and take care of the customers. You take care of you."

"Whad about da lake? Yer grandmudder's cottage?"

"My sister took off for two days. I can take off for a

day and a half. As she said, if the cottage isn't on the market in two weeks, no big deal. Besides, it looks like she may be moving to Grand Rapids. Maybe she'll want to keep it."

"If yer sure." Joan hesitated only a moment. Another sneeze convinced her. Picking up her box of tissues, she started for the back room where they kept their purses. At the doorway, she paused. "Diane's com'bing in at four."

"Good."

"Yer not like yer father, ya know." She managed a smile. "I'll be back damorrow."

The way Joan looked, Effie doubted her partner would be better in twenty-four hours. "You are not to step foot into this shop until Friday. Understood?"

"Bud—"

"No buts." She put on as stern a look as she could muster. "The others and I can cover this place for a couple of days while you get over that cold."

She had a feeling Joan wanted to argue, but another sneezing spell finalized Effie's point. Joan got her purse, gave the parrot and Mopsy good-bye pats, and headed for the door, promising she would call later. Laughter filled the shop as Joan left. Smiling, their one customer neared the counter, a package of invitations in her hand, along with matching paper plates, napkins, and cups. "She sounded terrible," the woman said. "I hate summer colds. Are these twenty percent off?"

Effie glanced at the price. "That's what it says."

Ten minutes later Effie was alone, looking over the week's work schedule. Besides her and Joan, they had three part-time employees. Joan had scheduled herself to open Wednesday and Thursday and to close on Friday. Although she'd told Joan not to come back to work until Friday, Effie knew she couldn't stay away from the lake that long. Much as she would like to avoid seeing Parker with Bern, it was inevitable. She needed to find someone to open Thursday.

The sound of laughter once again filled the room and the parrot squawked, telling her someone had entered the shop. Effie looked up, smiling a welcome. Immediately, she swallowed the smile. Seeing Parker was not only inevitable, it was happening.

He walked directly toward her, his white shirt and gray slacks wrinkled from wear and a stubble of beard on his chin. His gaze accused and so did his words. "Where were you last night?"

"Where was I?" She couldn't think straight. He wasn't supposed to be here, in her shop. He was supposed to be with her sister at the lake.

"Don't tell me at your apartment because I know you weren't, at least not before midnight."

"You were in my apartment?"

"Not in—at. Sitting on the steps. Parked in front of. I finally left after a patrol car cruised by for a second look. I wasn't sure how I would explain why I was there at that hour of the night."

"You drove down from the lake last night and parked in front of my apartment?"

"And then found a motel, which didn't even have courtesy razors." He rubbed a hand over the stubble on his jaw.

The action distracted Effie, but only for a moment. "Why? Why are you here at all? You and my sister should be—"

"Be what? We were back at the lake by five o'clock Tuesday evening. In fact, I was going to see if you wanted to go out to dinner. But what do I find? That you've taken off, gone to see some guy named Bubbles. There's no note. No explanation."

"I left a note."

"For your sister. I get a plastic bag with my shirt. I just don't understand you, Effie."

"Then let me explain." Effie scowled at him. He was trying to make her feel guilty, but she wasn't the one playing games. "I told you I didn't have class. I'm not even sophisticated enough to play 'switch partners.' I'm one of those old-fashioned types who feels if you make a date with one woman, you shouldn't break it to go out with another. And if you sleep with one sister one night, you shouldn't sleep with the other the—"

Parker didn't let her finish. "I didn't sleep with your sister last night. I know she gave you the idea that I would, but she was wrong. And I'm sorry about breaking our date. I just—" He wasn't sure how to explain that after telling her Tuesday morning that the stores didn't have a hold on him. Sighing, he apologized. "I'm sorry."

She shook her head. "The horseback ride doesn't matter. It doesn't even matter that you didn't sleep with Bern. What matters is she still likes you. I can't steal my sister's boyfriend."

"In other words, if Bern wants me, you walk away?" He'd hoped she had stronger feelings for him than that. "The other night was just a way of passing time?"

"I didn't say that." She looked away.

"Bern knows about us."

That got her attention. She looked back so quickly, he thought her neck would snap. "What do you mean, 'She knows about us'?"

"I told her."

"You told her we'd made love?"

"Not exactly." He smiled slightly. "Though I imagine she figured that out as easily as she guessed why I kept asking questions about you."

"And what did she say?"

"That she was happy for us."

"Of course she'd say that. What else could she say when you're about to become her boss?" Effie sent him an accusing glare. "You are going to give her the job, aren't you?"

"Yes, I'm going to give her the job."

"Good."

"Speaking of good, Bern said you'd be good for me."

"And you figured that meant she didn't care?" Effie knew her sister. Bern had been acting, for Parker's sake. She was a consummate actress, capable of hiding her emotions.

"She gave me directions to your apartment. Gave me your phone number."

"That doesn't mean she doesn't still like you . . . want you. Women learn how to cover up the hurts. Bern learned the lesson well. My father was a great teacher."

"And what did you learn from your father, Effie? To run from your emotions? To hide?"

"I learned not to trust anyone. That people let you down."

"Like me, in other words. Like your grandparents."

"My grandparents were the only ones who didn't let me down."

"They died, didn't they?"

"They were old. They couldn't live forever."

"You say that, but do you believe it? When you decided not to stop by the nursing home, did you expect your grandmother to die that night?"

"She'd said—that is, I knew—" Effie stopped. In a twisted way, she realized, Parker was right. There *had* been times when she'd blamed her grandmother for dying that night. And that blame was tied up with her guilt.

"Grow up, Effie. We're all human. We make mistakes, let people down. I'm sorry I let you down yesterday. I'm sorry I let my father down. I've been carrying my guilt around for years, killing myself by trying to make it up to him. Well, you're wrong about my not being able to let go of the business. I can. That's why I'm hiring Bern. And if she doesn't work out, I'll sell the business."

"Just like that?" She snapped her fingers, pinning him with a look.

"Just like that." He snapped his own fingers.

She knew better. "You'll never do it."

"You feel you know me so well, you can tell me what I will or will not do?"

"I know how your father was, and like it or not, you're like your father. You're like my father. Every time he came to see us, he'd promise to quit working in the field and take a job here in the States. It never happened."

"In other words, if I want you, I have to give up the stores?"

That wasn't what she meant. He was twisting her words. "What I want is a man who's there when I need him."

Laughter broke out and both the parrot and Mopsy added to the commotion. Effie glanced up to see two women and a preschooler entering the shop. She forced a smile of welcome, then brought her attention back to Parker. Like two combatants, they faced each other, neither looking away. Her mind suggested and discarded dozens of thoughts she wanted to convey. How did you

tell a man that you loved him, but it wouldn't work because you wanted more than he could ever give?

Parker's sigh broke the silence. "Are you going to
make Bernadette take care of everything at the lake?"

"No." Effie swallowed the tears that threatened to
embarrass her. "I was going back this morning, but
when I stopped by here, I found my partner sick and
sent her home. I've got to revamp the work schedule for
tomorrow, then when the woman who's going to close
today shows up, I'll take off. I should be there by five."

"I'll tell Bern."

"Thank you." They were so civil, it was sickening.
Here he was, about to leave her, and she couldn't tell
him how she felt. She loved him, and she was pushing
him away.

He headed for the door. Effie noticed the two
women watching him. The one without the child whispered something to the other, then spoke up. "Excuse
me." She directed her words toward Parker.

He looked at her, frowning.

"Aren't you Parker Morgan . . . the one on those
television ads?"

Parker hesitated a moment, his gaze going to Effie,
then he turned back to the woman. "Yes."

The woman smiled. "I want you to know, I drive all
the way to Grand Rapids just to shop at your store. Is it
true you may be opening one here in Kalamazoo?"

Again, Parker glanced at Effie. Her expression revealed nothing, but he could imagine her thoughts. She
wanted him to give up the business for her. Well, she
could forget that. For the last two years he'd been working day and night to get a store in Kalamazoo. Neither a
stress attack nor one good night of sex was enough reason to abandon that project.

His answer to the woman was his usual public-relations response. "It's true. We think sixty miles is too far for you to have to drive for the service and goods Morgan's prides itself in providing."

"That's great." The woman grinned at her companion, then back at him. "I'd like to say I really enjoy your ads too." A blush tinged her cheeks. "You could sell me anything anytime."

"Seems that doesn't hold true for everyone." He looked at Effie and knew she understood his meaning. Her expression didn't change, but she glanced away.

Laughter sounded when he opened the door. The recording didn't echo his heart.

TWELVE

Parker wasn't at the lake when Effie returned. Neither was Bernadette. Effie assumed they were together. At seven o'clock Bern returned, and Effie discovered she'd made another erroneous assumption.

"I've been over visiting Cindy," Bern said.

Her expression told Effie she hadn't been prepared for the physical changes in her friend. "Kind of a shock, isn't it?" Effie said. "When I first saw her, my mouth almost hit the floor. How's Mandy doing?"

"Not well. I guess the medication's not working as they'd hoped. Cindy's afraid she's going to have to take her into the doctor's tomorrow. I didn't realize how sick her girl was. She doesn't even have one completely functional kidney."

"And we think we have problems. I'm going to take her over a couple of the clown figures Grandma gave me."

"She'll like that. I feel bad about not calling Cindy. Not writing to her." Bern glanced out the window. "Did Parker come back with you?"

The question surprised Effie. "The last time I saw

him was this morning. To be honest, I thought he was with you."

Bern shook her head. "He called—on his cellular phone, I think—and said you'd be back this evening, but I haven't seen him since he took off last night, looking for you." She smiled knowingly. "I assume he found you."

"This morning. At the shop." Effie wished she could forget that confrontation. "He was quite upset, and we argued."

"He left here upset." She paused dramatically then went on. "You should have told me you two had gotten together."

The guilt Effie had been carrying lay like a weight on her shoulders. "I never should have let it happen."

An arching of eyebrows expressed Bern's surprise. "Why not? Don't you like him?"

"That's not the point. What I did was . . . Well . . ." She didn't know how to explain. "I'm sorry."

"There's nothing to be sorry for." Bern came to her, wrapping an arm around her shoulders. "Effie, I think it's great. You'll be good for him, and he'll be good for you. I remember him once saying you were like a beam of sunlight, and even as a teenager, you had a crush on him."

"But what about you?"

"What about me?" Bern gave her a keen look. "What? You're afraid I'm upset? Heartbroken?"

"Yesterday, you said—"

"A lot of things." Sisterly, she patted Effie's shoulder. "You should know by now you can't believe everything I say. Sure, if Parker had shown any interest, I was willing. The man still has a ton of sex appeal. I never should have dropped him thirteen years ago."

Effie needed to know. "He said he broke up with you."

Bern's frown was quick, then she grinned. "He broke up with me. I broke up with him. Does it matter?"

Only that Effie now knew the night he'd kissed her on the dock, he hadn't been salving a wounded ego. She also knew he'd told her the truth. But in the long run, it didn't matter. "No," she answered. "I made sure of that this morning."

Once again, Bernadette frowned. "How's that?"

"I backed him into a corner. Basically, I said it's me or the stores."

"You want him to give up Morgan's Department Stores?"

"No." Effie pulled away from her sister and walked across the room. "I don't know what I want." Stopping, she looked back. "I want a man who will put me first. Someone who loves me enough to be there when I need him. Is that wrong?"

"No, that's not wrong. I think we both want that."

"Well, somehow when I said it this morning, it didn't come out right." Shaking her head, she tried not to cry. "I didn't say anything right. I'd thought he would be with you. When he walked into the shop—"

Bern crossed over to her and gave her another comforting hug. "Effie, don't give up. The way he kept asking me questions about you yesterday, I'm certain he'll be back. I wouldn't be surprised if the man was in love with you."

Effie knew better than that. "I was a diversion. He was bored, you weren't here, and—"

"*And* nothing. The look I saw in his eyes when he talked about you, and the way he took off last night, like a streak of lightning . . ." Laughter infused Bern's words. "Effie, it's not boredom twitching that man's libido, it's you. Don't give up. He'll be back."

Thursday morning, Parker looked out over the main floor of the Twenty-eight Street store. Stopping in yesterday afternoon had been a mistake. Effie was right, he couldn't let go. Here he was, supposedly taking a two-week vacation, and in the last seven days he'd been in at least one of his two stores a total of five times. Six, if you considered yesterday and today as two times.

"Mr. Morgan?"

A woman in her early twenties approached him. He recognized her as the new hire in the lingerie department. Though they'd been introduced, he had to look at her name tag to remember her name. "Amy?"

She stopped in front of him. "The scanner on register twelve still isn't working right. I just had another customer complain."

"Same problem?"

"Exactly the same. She had one of our sale items. It was marked down on the rack, but when I ran it through, it came up full price."

"And you're sure the item was supposed to be on that rack?"

Amy nodded. "It's the same as what happened yesterday."

Which was why he was there. "Okay. We'll check it out again."

Let go, a voice in his head cried. Parker ignored the message and headed for the back offices. How could he let go? If it wasn't one problem, it was another. Effie didn't understand. You didn't just walk way from problems, from a legacy.

Except, as his doctor had said, he had to or he was going to kill himself.

Parker pushed open the door to the computer room. Taking a vacation at the lake had been a mistake. He was too close to the stores. It was too easy to stop by.

Yet, if he hadn't gone to the lake, he wouldn't have seen Effie again, wouldn't have felt the warmth of her smiles or the joy of her laughter. Wouldn't have made love with her.

He frowned, shaking his head. If he hadn't gone to the lake, his insides wouldn't be twisted in knots, and instead of thinking about a woman, he would be able to concentrate on the problems they were having with the computerized scanning system. He glanced around the room, looking for his programmer. "Jason?"

Love, Effie decided, didn't make the world go round, it caused mental earthquakes. "It messes up a person's thinking," she said early Friday morning, as she and Bernadette set up the tables for the yard sale. "There he was, the man of my dreams. He wanted me, and I put up every barrier you could imagine. Now he's gone."

Bern glanced toward Parker's cottage. "He'll be back. He said he'd be here today."

Said it to Bern when he'd called the day before. Effie knew there was no way Parker could have known she'd be away at exactly that time; still, she felt as though he'd shunned her. "Even if he comes back, it's not going to matter. Not after what I said to him Wednesday."

"You don't know that."

"I know what I said was true. He's tied to those stores. That call he made to you yesterday confirmed it.

Here he's supposed to be on a vacation, but where is he? At his store, working on some computer system."

"Because they were having problems with their scanners. Until I'm onboard and know what I'm doing, that's the way it will have to be. That doesn't mean it's the way it will always be."

Effie wasn't convinced things would change once Bern took over as general manager. "It's ingrained in him. Don't you remember the things his parents used to tell him? What amazes me is he went to New York. That must have really been a blow to them. You know, it's cruel, but I wonder if his father didn't die just to get Parker back."

Bern's frown brought an immediate response from Effie. "I know. I'm sick. Still, that man wanted his son running those stores. Every conversation I ever heard him have with Parker was about the business."

"That's all his parents talked about to me too." Bern straightened the kitchen utensils she'd laid out on one table. "I found it fascinating."

"You would." Effie hadn't. "That's why I always thought you and Parker were perfect for each other."

"So what are you saying, Effie? That you're not interested in Parker? That he can go jump into the lake?"

"I'm saying . . ." She glanced at his cottage. Wednesday night, all day Thursday, and all last night, she'd kept looking in that direction, wishing she'd see Parker. She'd as much as told him to get lost, but she was the one who was lost. "I'm saying it wouldn't work." That was the sad truth. "Morgan's Department Stores will always come before me."

"Effie, the reason he's hiring me is so he can get away more. He's trying to let go. On the other hand, you can't expect him to completely turn his back on a business that's been in his family for three generations."

"Can't I?" Effie shook her head, knowing the request was unreasonable. "He told me to grow up. Maybe that's my problem. Maybe I can't."

Bernadette brushed her hand over the clown costume lying on the table next to her. "You're giving up one of your childhood dreams here."

"Giving up a dream or running away again?"

Bern lifted the green tackle box Effie used for her clown makeup and gave her a questioning look. "Sell it or wait and see how you feel in a few more weeks?"

Inside the box were facial paints, mascara, lipstick, sparkles, baby powder, baby oil, glues, eyelashes, a wig, and her fake nose. A complete camouflage. A way for Effie Sanders to hide under the guise of Effie the Effervescent. Hide from the hurt and the loneliness of abandonment, escape from the pain inside. Laugh, and the world laughs with you.

Well, she could no longer laugh.

"Sell it. Sell it all."

At the intersection of Marsh Road and England Drive was a yard-sale sign with an arrow pointing the way to the Sanderses' cottage. Farther down the road, another sign and an array of colorful balloons announced exactly where the sale was being held. Two unfamiliar cars were parked in front of the Sanderses' cottage—a newer-model Chevy and an old junky Jeep—and Parker could see two women and a couple of teenagers pawing through the items piled on the picnic and card tables Bern and Effie had set on the small patch of lawn between the road and their cottage.

He parked in front of his place and slowly got out of his car. Bern was standing behind one table, talking with the two women, but Effie stood back by the cottage.

Her gaze was on him, holding him. He wasn't sure what to do. Smile? Wave?

He did neither.

Two days had passed since he'd seen her. Three since he'd made love with her. When he'd walked out of her shop Wednesday, he'd told himself forgetting her would be easy. As easy as it had been with all of the other women he'd slept with in the last thirteen years.

Well, he'd been wrong. He hadn't forgotten her. He hadn't been able to get her out of his mind. Awake or asleep, he'd been haunted by her. Every laugh he heard brought back memories of her laughter. Another woman's smile reminded him of how much he loved Effie's smiles, loved the dimples in her cheeks. He yearned to touch her again, to smell the sweet, feminine scent of her body. He longed to hold her close. Talk to her. Make love with her. Simply looking at Effie caused a tightening in his loins and a twisting in his gut.

He wasn't sure what to do, but if he had to sell the stores to get her, then Gene Hill had a deal.

Effie looked away, and he sucked in a breath. What he said in the next few minutes could either bring her back into his arms or send her away. The tightening in his loins was matched by a tightening in his chest, and he forced himself to breathe deeply. Even if it gave him a heart attack, he had to go talk to her.

From the time the two teenage boys had gotten out of their Jeep, Effie had kept close tabs on them. There was something about the way they kept sneaking furtive looks at each other and smiling that made her uneasy. But the moment she saw Parker's car coming down the road, her attention had switched to him.

Even not looking his way, she knew he was walking

toward her. She braced herself for a confrontation, all the while wanting to run to his arms and welcome him back. For a night and a morning, he'd made her complete. She'd tasted love. The next few minutes might determine if she ever tasted it again.

"How's it going?" he asked as he neared.

She looked his way, not bothering to pretend she was surprised to see him. "Not bad. We've already sold quite a bit."

Bernadette called to him. "Did you get that problem at the store resolved?"

"All taken care of," he answered her. "Took until late last night, however, to find the glitch." His gaze came back to Effie. "I called yesterday."

"So Bern said."

"You were at the store?"

He made it a question. She gave him an answer. "Getting supplies to make the signs we put up."

Parker lowered his voice. "We need to talk."

The phone rang inside the cottage. Bern glanced their way and smiled. "I'll get it."

Her sister was trying to get them together, and Effie appreciated the effort. Not that this was the time to talk. There was too much to say, and too many people around. She stepped away from Parker, moving closer to the table that held her clown paraphernalia.

He followed her, picking up the baggy clown pants with their sparkling sequins. "You're going to sell it?"

"There's no use hanging on to it." The sunlight made the sequins shimmer, and she looked away. "I can't put it on without remembering what I did—what I didn't do."

"And I can't help feeling your grandmother would be disappointed in you."

"Seems I'm disappointing a lot of people."

He set the pants down. "Makes us a pair, doesn't it?"

The pain she heard in his voice surprised her. She'd expected anger—or indifference. She didn't move when he touched her cheek with the backs of his fingers, but the caress brought unexpected tears to her eyes and caught her breath in her throat.

"I want you," he whispered, too low for the boys at the tables to hear.

"Effie—" Bern's call clashed with the emotions pouring through her. "It's Cindy. She wants to talk to you."

Never looking away from Parker, Effie yelled back. "I'll call her later."

"She's at the hospital . . . in Grand Rapids. She's nearly hysterical. I think she said Mandy has to be operated on, but is refusing and carrying on so much, they're afraid if they do operate she won't make it. Cindy thinks you might be able to help."

"Me? How?"

"I don't know." Bern waved her in. "Come talk to her."

Effie glanced at Parker. His expression clearly stated his feelings. He expected her to take the call. Knowing what Cindy was going to ask, Effie turned toward the house.

"I can't," Effie said, squeezing her eyes shut to block out Cindy's plea.

Understanding Cindy had been difficult. Her sometimes incoherent words were mingled with sobs, her thoughts jumping from one subject to another. Cindy's message, however, was clear. Her daughter would die if she went into this operation in her present state of mind. Amanda Nelson's will to live was gone.

Cindy was grasping at straws, looking for a miracle. Effie didn't feel she could provide that miracle. "You don't know that she'll respond to a clown."

The sound of Parker's voice brought Effie back to what was going on in the kitchen. The boys, he'd said, were leaving, they hadn't bought anything, and one of the women wanted to know the price of a table.

"I'll take care of her," Bern said, leaving Parker where he stood.

His look stole Effie's thoughts, and she missed the last of what Cindy said. The silence on the line, however, signaled Cindy was waiting for an answer. Effie responded to what Cindy had said earlier. "I know she liked Mopsy."

Parker's look judged her. He wouldn't have this dilemma, she knew. He would go.

All she did was disappoint.

Others.

Herself.

"Please—"

Cindy's plea rang in her ear, tearing at her heart. How could she say no? How could she refuse a desperate mother? Why hadn't she gone that night her grandmother had wanted to see her?

Again, she closed her eyes, hearing the voice of the nurse in the home. "She waited up for you. She was sure you'd come."

"I—"

The words wouldn't come, the emotions pouring through Effie in a swirl of confusion. The touch of a hand on her arm opened her eyes, and she looked up at Parker's face. He didn't speak, but he asked, and she knew she couldn't refuse.

"I'll be there," she said quietly, a sense of calm passing through her once the decision was made. "I'll be there with Mopsy. It will take me a little while to get my makeup and costume on, but tell Mandy that Effie the Effervescent is on her way."

Effie slowly placed the receiver back on the phone, her gaze locked with Parker's. His look warmed her, his touch giving her the strength she needed. She could do it.

The sound of Bernadette yelling intruded on Effie's feelings of triumph.

She knew Bern wouldn't yell unless there was a problem, and so did Parker. He moved as quickly as she did, leading the way out of the cottage. Effie stopped when she saw Bern standing by the edge of the road, shaking a fist. Parker spoke first. "What happened?"

Bern faced them, her eyes snapping with anger. "They ripped us off."

Parker kept walking toward. her. "Who ripped you off?"

"Those boys. They came back, and one grabbed Grandpa's fishing rods and ice awl while the other got Grandma's coin collection and—" She looked at Effie. "They took the tackle box with your clown makeup. They must have thought it held fishing tackle."

Effie gasped a no, and Parker looked down the road in the direction Bern had been shaking her fist. "They went that way?"

"Yes." She followed his gaze, still frowning.

"Which means they're heading out to the end of England Point. If they're not from around here, they may not realize the only way off this peninsula is this road, and that it simply loops around."

The minute Parker stepped into the middle of the road, Effie understood his intent. The way the trees grew and the cottages had been built, what started as two lanes, where England Drive intersected the main road, turned into one lane at this point. A man standing in the middle did create a blockade. At least, that's what it looked like Parker intended on doing.

Effie ran toward him, knowing nothing, not even the clown makeup, was worth his risking his life. "Parker, don't."

She heard the Jeep before she saw it, the muffler roaring its approach. Parker glared at her. "Stay back."

He spread his arms to widen his dimensions, but the Jeep didn't slow. Effie watched it approach, and her actions were automatic, conditioned by months of repetitive practice. Standing on the edge of the road, she reached out, capturing Parker's arm between the palms of her hands. "Roll back," she heard her instructor chant in her mind, and in a flowing, circular motion, she brought her weight back, dragging Parker's arm with her.

Unprepared, he didn't resist, his body following the flow of her motion. He passed in front of her just as the Jeep sped by, never swerving. Together, they watched the car race on toward the intersection.

Parker moved first, turning away from her without a word. In a second, she knew where he was headed and called after him. "Wait for me."

"Hurry," he yelled, opening his car door.

She slipped into the passenger seat as he shoved the gear into reverse. Her door swung shut as he backed up. They were at the end of the road before she had her seat belt on. She saw the Jeep first, speeding away. "To the right."

Parker turned in that direction, surging out in front of an approaching car. "Dial nine-one-one." He pointed at the cellular phone lying on the console between them. "Tell them those kids almost ran me down."

As soon as they were on 124th, Parker passed a car and closed in on the Jeep. Effie's message to the dispatcher who took her call was cryptic. She knew saying the situation was a matter of life and death was overly dramatic, but in a way it was true. Only she and Parker understood how important that makeup was at this moment.

The Jeep turned right again, onto a dirt road, and Parker followed, slowly closing the distance. A third right turn put them temporarily on pavement, but then a left brought them back to dirt. Parker kept inching closer, and all the while Effie kept talking into the phone, informing the dispatcher of their progress and avoiding any definitive answers as to what the boys had stolen.

"Damn!" Parker swore and braked to turn down a two-track path through a field of soybeans. "This car wasn't built for off-road driving. Tell them to hurry."

She gave the new directions and as complete a description of the Jeep and the boys as she could. The dispatcher assured her that help was on the way. Effie saw the Jeep head off the path and across the soybean field, and knew Parker couldn't follow. He slowed his car, then put on the brakes, once again swearing.

They watched the Jeep bounce over row after row of bean plants, traveling farther and farther away. "You can almost hear them laughing," she said, angered that the boys were getting away.

"They're crazy," Parker said. "I shouldn't have trusted them, should have waited until they'd actually driven away before I came inside your place. The way they were acting, I should have—"

Parker stopped. Either his eyes were going bad, or

the Jeep wasn't moving forward anymore. He could see the dirt kicking up behind its wheels, but its position in the field compared with the tree line along the side hadn't changed. Curious, he opened his door.

He knew Effie was following as he ran across the field toward the Jeep. He also knew she'd saved his life earlier. The one who was crazy was him, thinking he could stop a car by holding out his arms.

The furrows made his progress difficult, and he wasn't in shape, but he was glad the doctor had insisted he start exercising. The pounding of his heart didn't scare him as it would have only two months ago. Heck, he'd almost gotten himself run over. A little pressure in his lungs wasn't anything.

The closer he drew to the Jeep, the clearer he could see what was going on. It wasn't dirt but mud the Jeep's tires were kicking up. The car was being rocked back and forth in a valiant attempt to free it, but the opposite was occurring, each reversal miring the Jeep deeper.

Parker knew when the boys saw him. Both the driver's door and the passenger's door flew open at the same time, the two kids bailing out and taking off in opposite directions. He went after the driver, a new surge of adrenaline pushing him on. Only when Effie called after him did he slow.

Looking back, he saw her by the Jeep, holding a green tackle box above her head. Then she waved back toward his car. The flashing lights of two patrol cars announced the arrival of the cavalry. Parker walked back toward Effie, his breathing labored and his legs heavy, but feeling very much alive.

THIRTEEN

Parker kept his gaze on the flashing lights of the patrol car ahead and his foot on the accelerator, but once in a while he glanced in the rearview mirror, following Effie's progress in the backseat as she changed from the woman he knew to a clown. "Do you realize," he said, "It was one week ago today that I looked out my kitchen window and saw you doing your tai chi exercises."

"Bet you didn't think one week later you'd be heading down a freeway doing eighty miles an hour while a clown put on her makeup. Don't hit any bumps or Effie the Effervescent's smile is going to become a smirk."

"For some reason, the moment I saw you, I knew you were going to change my life."

"Right. Tell me. What did you really think when you saw me?"

"The honest truth?" He wasn't sure he remembered.

"The honest truth."

"That you'd grown up."

"And?"

"That I wanted to make love with you."

"Oh, I'm sure."

The scent of baby powder filled the car, and he chanced another glance in the mirror. Effie had set her makeup with the powder and was now applying eyelashes that practically covered her forehead. Her cheeks were chalk white and her nose had become a bulbous red ball. She looked up and caught him watching, and he gave his answer. "I'm sure."

"Still want to make love with me?"

He didn't hesitate. "Yes."

"You're crazy, you know."

He turned his attention back to the road and the patrol car ahead. Crazy did describe his recent mental state. "I think it's something that happens to me when I'm around you. I take off for New York. Jump in front of speeding cars." Simply thinking about what he'd done caused his stomach to tighten. "I can't believe I actually stood in the middle of that road and tried to stop those kids with my body."

"You scared the life out of me."

He remembered feeling her hands pressing on opposite sides of his arm. It hadn't seemed as though she were holding him tightly. It hadn't even seemed as if she were really pulling him. He'd simply felt himself moving, her body and his blending, completing a circle. He couldn't explain it. He only knew her actions had probably saved his life. "I never thanked you."

"Thank my tai chi instructor. He said, 'If you practice the moves over and over, after a while you won't even think about them or what you're doing, you'll just do it.' So I practiced. Over and over. And he was right. I just did it."

"Practiced pulling people out of roads?"

"No. I practiced 'ward off' and 'roll back.' That's all I did today, just those two moves. And they worked."

"But you didn't ward me off. You pulled me around like a rag doll." He checked her progress. She looked like a rag doll. She'd put on her wig, which covered her curls as well as her ears. The red yak hair had a brassiness missing in her natural color and was laced with sequins.

He knew from what she'd told him that when she was finished, her entire body would be covered, either with clothing or makeup. She was changing before his eyes. The woman he'd made love with was becoming a "joey," and just in time, it seemed. "We're almost there."

His cellular phone rang. From the back seat, Mopsy barked and poked her nose between the seats, sniffing at the case. He picked up the phone. "Probably that deputy up ahead checking on your progress."

Effie put the last of her makeup away and looked around the backseat for her gloves. When she stepped out of the car, she would be in full costume. Not that it had been easy getting dressed in a moving car. If she hadn't used the "life and death" bit on the sheriff, she might have taken the time to change and put on her makeup at the cottage. But getting the officers to let her and Parker leave the bean field without answering a ton of questions had taken some fast talking and dramatic action. Best of all, one of the deputies had known about Cindy and Mandy. He was the one escorting them to the hospital. He'd gone with them back to the cottage, had waited while she'd picked up the rest of her costume and washed the mud from her feet and legs, then he'd led the way down 124th to I-131 and north to Grand Rapids.

"What do you mean he quit?"

Parker's tone caught her attention more than his

words. She scooted to the side so she could see his profile. He wasn't smiling.

"No, I can't come in," he said into the phone.

Effie watched the patrol car slow to a stop ahead of them. They'd reached the hospital in record time. In one of the rooms, a little girl waited. Effie looked up the side of the building, but her attention was on what Parker was saying.

Irritation laced his words. "That store is going to have to function without me."

He gave her a weak smile, but she could tell he was listening to the caller, and she knew what would happen next. He would give his excuses and he would leave her. Duty called. He was needed at the store.

No matter that she needed him.

The sheriff's deputy got out of his car and started back toward them. Parker covered the mouthpiece of the phone. "You go on in. I'll be there in a minute."

She knew he wouldn't be. He'd never be there, not when it counted. She'd grown up waiting for her father to appear. She wasn't going to spend the rest of her life waiting for another man. "Go on," she said, nodding toward the phone. "Take care of business."

He lifted his eyebrows, then spoke into the mouthpiece. "Just a minute."

The deputy opened her door, and Effie scooped up Mopsy, slipping her into one of the oversized pockets of her costume. The touch of her hand on the dog's head would keep Mopsy quiet and out of sight until it was time for her to appear. Swallowing back tears of disappointment, Effie stepped out of the car and dashed for the hospital's entrance.

❖――――――❖

"And now, ladies and gentlemen." Cindy waved her hands with a flourish, her gaze on her daughter. "If you'll direct your attention toward the main arena."

Mandy turned her head toward the hospital-room door, her eyes wide with expectation but looking more sunken than Effie remembered. Plastic tubes ran from hanging containers of fluid to the child's thin arms while a monitor beeped in an eerie rhythm. Effie forced a smile to match the one painted on her face and bounced into the room. "Tah-dah!"

She pirouetted at the end of the bed and just to the side so Mandy could see, bowed low, then pulled her hand from her pocket. On cue, Mopsy poked out her head, the red-and-gold bow tied to the hair between her ears flopping ridiculously to the side. With a bark, Mopsy greeted Mandy.

The child's squeal of delight was weak but welcome. Effie removed Mopsy from her pocket, setting the dog on the linoleum floor by the bed. Mandy tried to sit up to see, and the nurse by her side quickly offered assistance, supporting her while another nurse elevated the bed.

Mandy turned to the nurse by her side. "I know this clown. This dog was at my grandma's." She looked at Effie. "Make her do her tricks."

Effie blew into her wooden whistle, and Mopsy obeyed. The act had begun, the gag almost second nature to the two of them. Only when she turned, facing the door, did Effie falter. Parker was standing there, and she stared at him, unsure if she really believed her eyes.

He was here, at the hospital. He was stepping into Mandy's room. He hadn't gone to his store, hadn't left her.

Her smile blossomed.

Searching high and low, she poked around Mandy's

bed, ignoring the child's directions on where Mopsy was hiding. Effie played the fool and loved it. She was a fool. A fool in love with a man who'd had the gumption to follow his dreams, if only for a little while; a man who understood how a selfish act could leave you feeling so guilty you would abandon your dreams. He was here, when she needed him, and he'd been ready to do battle for her with just his bare hands. He was crazy and wonderful, exciting and sexy.

She glanced his way, needing to assure herself he hadn't disappeared. He formed an okay sign with his fingers and thumb, and she went on with the act. Dropping to her knees on the linoleum, she was glad for the knee pads under her baggy trousers. Mopsy hopped on her back, and Effie carefully rose to her feet, still pretending to look for the dog.

Mandy laughed, the sound even weaker than before, and Effie brought the gag to a close, knowing nothing would be accomplished if Mandy was too exhausted to survive the operation. Mopsy back in her pocket, Effie approached the bed and took Mandy's hand in hers. "I understand you're not feeling well."

Mandy nodded solemnly. "My plumbing doesn't work."

The simplistic answer said it all. If only the solution were as easy. "So why don't you let them fix your plumbing?"

"They said they had." Mandy looked at her mother. "They promised I wouldn't have to have another operation."

Effie knew how sorry Cindy was for making that promise. Gently, she brought Mandy's attention back to her. "Sometimes people make promises they can't keep. Things don't always go as expected. The doctors just want to make you feel better. That's why they want to try again."

"But it hurts." Mandy whimpered, tears filling her eyes. "I don't want it to hurt anymore."

"None of us like to hurt." Wishing she could take away the pain, she stroked the back of Mandy's hand. "But you know, we all do, sometime or another. Even clowns hurt."

"And clown dogs?" Mandy pulled away from Effie's touch to reach for Mopsy.

A glance at one of the nurses and the woman's nod brought Mopsy from Effie's pocket to Mandy's bed. As if sensing Mandy's delicate condition, Mopsy quietly lay down beside the child and licked the hand patting her head. Mandy's smile was truly effervescent, her eyes bright.

Effie thought fast. "How would you like to teach Mopsy a new trick?"

"Me?" Mandy looked up, questioning the possibility. "Now?"

"Not now." She pointed at the IV in Mandy's arm. "That would get in the way. I'll make you a deal. You have this operation, get better, and then you and I will teach Mopsy a new trick."

"What kind of trick?"

"Whatever kind you want her to learn. Is it a deal?"

Mandy glanced at her mother, then at Mopsy. No one spoke, all waiting for Mandy's answer. Effie held her breath when Mandy looked back at her. "Will this be the last time I have to have an operation?"

"I can't make that promise, but I know the doctors are going to try real hard to make it right this time."

"So my plumbing will work?"

"So you can do all the things you want to do."

"I wanna be a clown."

"Then you can be a clown—or a doctor or a nurse. Can the nurse tell the doctor you're ready?"

Mandy didn't answer. All too serious for her age, she stared at Mopsy. Again, there was silence as they all waited for Mandy's answer.

It came as a question. "Will you be here when I wake up? You and Mopsy?"

"I'll be here," Effie promised, knowing she couldn't leave until she knew Mandy was all right.

"Then you can tell them I'm ready."

Parker sat beside Effie in the waiting room. In front of them, Cindy paced, going from the doorway to the television set and back again. Cindy's father sat facing the television, his eyes closed, while Cindy's mother thumbed through a magazine. They'd been waiting for four hours, the clock ticking away the minutes with agonizing slowness.

Effie's stomach growled, and Mopsy looked up from the chair she was lying on, cocking her head quizzically. Effie smiled, patting the front of her baggy trousers with a gloved hand.

Parker was also hungry. "Do you want something to eat?"

She shook her head. "I can't eat while in costume. But if you want something . . ."

"No." He'd forgotten the code of ethics she was obliged to observe, and he knew she wouldn't change out of her costume, not until Mandy was again awake and Effie's promise fulfilled. Promises were important to her. Promises made to her, and promises she made.

"You doing all right?" He trailed his gaze down her costume, wondering if the woman he'd made love to four nights ago was beneath the baggy clothing and sequins. "No problems or feelings of guilt?"

She looked away. "A few."

"She would be proud of you."

Effie glanced back and nodded. "I know."

"I'm proud of you."

She reached over and took his hand, her gloved fingers barely covering his. "And I'm proud of you."

Though the face that looked up at him was a bizarre caricature of the woman, in her eyes he saw the sparkle he'd grown to adore, and her voice held the gentleness that soothed and excited him. Down the hall, at the nurses' station, a telephone rang. Automatically, he looked that way.

"If you want to call the store—?" She hesitated, and he looked back. She shrugged. "Go to the store?"

"I'm on vacation."

She laughed, and both Cindy and her mother looked their way. Effie lowered her voice. "Some vacation."

Parker put a hand on her knee, needing to feel the real her. He found a knee pad. "It's had its ups and downs. More ups, since I met you."

A sidelong glance was all he got. "Are we still discussing vacations?"

"I'm not teaching you golf."

Inside of her painted smile, she grinned. "You did make a hole in one the other night."

"A couple of times. And you handled the balls quite well."

She looked around the room, checking that no one had overheard, and Parker could see a flush of color under her white makeup. Somehow, seducing a clown didn't seem right. On the other hand, he wanted Effie badly. "Got any plans for tonight?"

"We should go back to the lake. Help Bern."

That wasn't what he'd had in mind. "When I called her to let her know what was going on, she said she'd recruited a couple of the neighbor kids to help. She can get along without us until tomorrow. My apartment isn't far from here."

"We may not get out of here for a while yet."

He understood. The operation was taking longer than expected and it would be even longer before Mandy recovered enough to have visitors. How long they were there didn't bother him as much as Effie's reticence. "If you'd rather not . . ."

He wasn't sure, but he thought he heard her chuckle. The look she gave him, however, was purely innocent. "I will need somewhere to wash up and change."

"Am I all better?" Mandy asked, her eyes heavy with the sedation that would keep her from feeling any pain.

"The doctors think they got everything fixed this time," Cindy said, holding her daughter's hand. "At least until it's time for that *big* operation. Look who's here."

Effie moved closer, and Mandy smiled. "You did stay."

"We stayed."

"Mopsy too?"

"Mopsy too." Effie lifted the little dog from her pocket and held Mopsy close enough that Mandy could touch her paw. "And now we're going to go home and study the clown book on how to learn new tricks so when you feel all better, we'll be ready for whatever gag you want us to learn."

"Gag?"

"Trick."

"Can I be in the trick?"

"I don't see why not."

"Can I be a clown?"

Effie glanced at Cindy, then back at Mandy. "I don't see why not."

Mandy smiled, and Effie stepped away from the bed, slipping Mopsy back into her pocket. She waited a minute, to be certain her leaving would be all right. As Mandy's eyes drifted closed Effie knew the child was satisfied. Her promise had been kept. Now she had other promises to keep.

Turning away from the bed, she faced Parker.

Parker's apartment made Effie's look like a doghouse. She was reluctant to set Mopsy down on the plush white carpeting, even after having taken the dog out for several walks during their stay at the hospital. She looked at Parker. "I don't imagine pets are allowed in this building."

"There is a 'no pets' clause in the lease." He eased Mopsy from her hands and set the dog down. "But since I own the building, I wouldn't worry."

"I should have known." Effie slipped off her oversized shoes and cautiously walked around, investigating the apartment's layout. Rich browns, burnished golds, and off-whites were repeated in expensive fabrics, quality woods, and handcrafted metals. "Poor little rich boy."

"It's a rough life, but someone has to live it." He pointed down a short hallway. "Bathroom's that way."

She hesitated before leaving him. "That call today. The one you got in the car. You should have gone to the store. Right?"

"We have a couple of problems."

"And you could have solved them?"

"One. I'm not sure about the other. My manager quit this morning. For the second time in as many months, he made a decision."

"With Bernadette coming on board, does it matter?"

He nodded. "Ben is a good man. Not a good general manager, but a good man. He would have been valuable in another position. I just never got a chance to talk to him about it." Again, he waved a hand toward the hallway. "Go on. I don't want to talk about business. I want to find out if Effie Sanders really is hiding beneath all that paint and glitter."

She also wanted to get out of the costume and makeup, but she didn't move. "Maybe we need to talk about business. Parker, what I said the other day in my shop, I didn't mean you had to sell Morgan's. What you did today—being there when I needed you—that's all I want. You don't need to give up anything, and I definitely don't want you making any decisions you'll later regret."

"Whatever decisions I make, we'll make together." He smiled and reached forward, releasing the buttons for the straps of her trousers.

She watched the loose-fitting pants drop to her ankles, exposing her cotton socks and knee pads. "Shouldn't you go to your store now? Take care of those problems?"

He started on the buttons of her blouse. "What problems? Everyone's telling me to let go, to relax. I'm just following doctor's orders."

A button was released. Then another. Effie said nothing, did nothing. The way he was looking at her, devouring her with his eyes was enough. Only when her blouse was completely open and pushed back, exposing her bra, did she speak. "And are you relaxed?"

His lusty chuckle answered her question. He took her hand and brought it to him. Relaxed was not a word that would describe his condition.

"I should take off the makeup." Her voice sounded as shaky as she suddenly felt. "It might . . . We might . . ."

He smiled, again motioning down the hallway. "Be my guest."

Effie knew she looked ridiculous walking down the hallway holding her trousers up with one hand. She didn't look back. Parker's grin had been too seductive, his need too close to hers. In his bathroom, she closed the door and leaned back against it, taking in a deep breath and releasing it slowly.

He'd stayed at the hospital, he wanted her, and she wanted him. Life was wonderful. Love was wonderful.

She'd left her tackle box on the backseat of his car. For a moment she considered asking Parker to get it for her, then remembered the last time they'd shared space in a bathroom. Until she had her makeup off, she could be a disaster to his apartment.

She didn't find any baby oil in his cabinet, but there was some lotion, and between that and half a box of tissues, she removed the caked makeup. When she was finished, she showered, scrubbing the remaining traces of makeup and mud from her body. Only as she toweled herself dry did she remember her shorts and top were also lying on the backseat of his car. Not that she thought she would need them, at least not for a while.

She stepped out of his bathroom with a big, fluffy blue towel wrapped around her and her heart pounding in her chest. The silence in the apartment was eerie. A clock in his living room struck the hour, the six chimes cutting through her. When it finished, she called out his name.

FOURTEEN

Effie was about to call out a second time when she heard the click of the front door. Pulling the towel closer, she stepped back, ready to duck into the bathroom if it wasn't Parker. The tension evaporated from her body when Mopsy came trotting into the apartment, tail wagging. Parker followed. He grinned the moment he saw her. "There was a person under all that paint after all."

Stepping forward, she shook her head, her curls still damp. "Where did you two go?"

"For a walk." He closed the door behind him. "Your dog was acting hungry, so while you were in the shower, I gave her some hamburger. Then I got to thinking she might need to go out. So we went." He grimaced as he walked toward her. "I now know every inch of that lawn out back."

"She is particular. Just like her mama."

He stopped in front of her, again grinning. Between his thumb and forefinger, he caught a lock of her hair and rubbed the strands together. "Mama's starting to age . . . or this clown business is getting to you."

He showed her a bit of white on his finger, and she

understood. Try as she might to avoid it, she always got some makeup in her hair. Putting it on in the car had made things worse, and though she'd washed thoroughly and shampooed twice, she had a feeling she'd missed several places. She cocked her head to the side. "What about behind my ears?"

He brushed his thumb behind one ear, and she shivered. "Just a little."

"I'm like a kid." She gave him a view of the other. "You gotta check me behind the ears."

He traced a path behind that ear, then slid his hand down the side of her neck to her bare shoulder. "Not quite like a kid."

Effie looked up as the husky timbre of his voice sent a tremor through her. She definitely wasn't feeling like a kid, and the look in his eyes said he didn't see a kid. His gaze traveled down to the cleavage exposed above the towel, and his smile became more provocative. "Hungry?"

Five minutes earlier, she would have said she was starved. Now butterflies filled her stomach, a giddiness wiping out all thoughts of food. "Not really."

"Would you like to see my bedroom?"

A skip in the beat of her heart was her body's response. Verbally, she strove for a casual tone. "Sure."

How one man could twist her in knots so easily amazed Effie, but it had always been that way. As a teenager, she'd adored him, but in the last week, she'd seen him in a new light. He carried his guilt, just as she carried hers. They couldn't change the past, couldn't bring back his father or her grandmother, but in the last few hours, they'd both taken steps forward. She'd been the clown, and he'd resisted the pull of the store. What came next, she wasn't sure.

She stopped at the doorway to his bedroom, placing

a hand on his arm. He paused, and she looked up at him. "Where are we headed?"

He glanced into the room, at the king-size bed with its massive headboard, then back at her. "You want the answer I would have given most women at this moment, or the truth?"

"The truth."

"I don't know."

She looked away, longing for more yet knowing she was asking too much. He tilted her chin so she again had to look at him. "I want to make love to you, Effie. Now. Tonight. Tomorrow. And for a thousand tomorrows after that." He smiled. "You're kind of addictive, shrimp."

In spite of her concerns, she managed a smile of her own. "It's our small size. We sneak up on you."

"You didn't sneak. You hit me like tornado. Sent me spinning. I'm still spinning."

"You?" She shook her head. "I find that hard to believe."

He grinned and led her into the room. "There's a lot you don't know about me, Ms. Sanders. A lot I don't know about myself that I think you're going to teach me. That is, if you're interested."

He stopped beside his bed and waited for her answer. Effie said nothing, simply reached forward and began unbuttoning his shirt. Her interest went beyond teaching. A little experimenting seemed in order. Touching.

She spread his shirt apart, exposing the mat of brown hairs on his chest. His skin was warm to her touch. Soft. Sliding her hands down over his ribs to his waist, she pinched a roll of extra flesh.

He grunted. "That's going."

"They call them love handles."

"I've got another handle you can love."

"And I suppose you think I'm interested."

"Aren't you?"

She glanced down at the front of his slacks. Her insides were liquid with her interest, her heart racing, and her legs weak. She could tell by the slight bulge in his trousers that he shared her interest.

"I'll show you mine if you'll show me yours."

His low, seductive voice teased her. She tried to tease back. "I've already seen it, remember? Besides, I played that game once, when I was six. Grandma caught me."

"Big trouble." He ran his fingertips along the edge of her towel, where she'd wrapped it into itself. Traitorously the cloth gave way to his touch, the thick cotton sagging down and exposing her breasts, then falling to the floor.

Her breath caught in her throat when he touched her. With his fingers he caressed; with his eyes he devoured. "I'll never see enough of you."

"Parker, this is kind of scary for me." The trembling in her voice emphasized her words. "I don't think I can handle an affair with you."

"I don't think this is an affair."

"We've known each other such a short time."

"Sixteen years." With his thumbs, he circled her nipples, sliding across them just often enough to drive her crazy.

"We were apart thirteen of those sixteen years. You were in love with my sister." A point she couldn't forget.

"I was a boy. I didn't know about love." He eased her back on the bed, leaning over her. "You were still a child."

"Parker?" She knew what he was going to do before

his mouth touched her. The moist play of his tongue and gentle sucking of his lips created instant insanity. Nevertheless, she curled her fingers into his hair and pushed his head back, needing to say the words. "I may have been a child, but I was in love with you then, and I think I'm in love with you now."

He said nothing, simply stared at her, and she held her breath, afraid he would pull away. Even when he smiled, she didn't move. It was the brush of his finger across her lips, then his soft kiss that gave her hope.

"A woman told me once," he said, leaning back just enough to study her face, "that I was incapable of love, that the only important thing in my life was Morgan's Department Stores. Well, today I turned my back on Morgan's Department Stores."

"I know."

"I found something more important. You want to know where we're headed?" He smiled. "My guess is for the altar."

When he kissed her, Effie didn't hold back. Wrapping her arms around his neck, she pulled him down on her. The gabardine of his slacks was smooth against her bare skin, his belt buckle cold. She reached between them, loosening the buckle, and he took it from there, a few wiggles of his hips pushing his slacks to his knees. When he leaned against her again, it was only the soft cotton of his briefs that teased her . . . and what they covered.

His tongue played into her mouth and she grappled with it, giving him her tongue in return. Their kisses spoke of need and relief, a wanting tempered by the knowledge that this wasn't a fleeting moment, that what they were sharing would be shared over and over, night after night. Exploration became as necessary as arousal, a desire to find new places to touch and kiss, lave and nibble.

Each learned about the other, finding pleasure in the giving as well as the taking. Effie waited when he paused to remove his shoes and socks, then slip off his trousers and briefs. She tantalized him with words as her hands caressed. He'd shown her his, and she'd shown him hers, and together they found a fit.

In the ebbing light of the day, they created a rhythm uniquely their own yet as old as mankind. Two halves of a whole, again united. She knew it had been worth the wait. A day. A week. Thirteen years. It would always be worth the wait.

As a teenager, she'd dreamed of loving him. As a woman, she was ready. In her arms, he drove deeper and deeper, and she responded, arching her hips and taking him in. His breathing became labored, and she knew he wouldn't last long. She wasn't going to last long. The spasms were beginning, carrying her to the heights.

She cried out his name, and heard him groan hers. He was with her. Soaring. Together they would find happiness and fulfillment. Together, they could beat the world.

They stood naked in the wide space of flooring at the end of his bed. Side by side, they moved. She lifted her arms shoulder high, breathing in. He followed. Their arms came to their chests, then down. "Bird's tail right," Effie said, and crossed her hands to the right, stepping in that direction. Parker echoed her movements.

"Bird's tail left." A repeat.

"Ward off. Pull back. Push—"

Parker did each movement with her, watching and

smiling. He had a feeling not too many people learned tai chi this way. They were getting down to the *bare* essentials. But it certainly wasn't relaxing. Simply watching her move aroused him, and though they'd spent most of the night making love, the desire once again rose within him. He knew she could see the rise in another part of his body.

She glanced down at his hips and grinned. "We don't use the rod at this stage."

He grinned. "When do we use it?"

The ring of the telephone came before her answer. He lowered his hands and turned to his bedstand. Mopsy trotted across the bed to him, and he automatically stroked her head as he picked up his phone.

Effie stood where she was, waiting and watching him, and he hoped it wasn't another crisis at the store. He'd made a decision yesterday, one he didn't regret. Yet he couldn't completely turn his back on the stores. He would do what was necessary to keep them going, and going successfully. On the other hand, if it came to a choice between Effie and the stores, he knew which he would chose. Effie would always come first.

To his relief, it was Cindy. "I called Bern, and she gave me this number," she said.

Parker wasn't surprised. They'd called Bern last night, telling her they would be staying in Grand Rapids for the night and would be coming out to help her in the morning. Not that Bern seemed to care. The neighbor children, she'd said, were working out fine, and she had them scheduled to help this morning too.

Bernadette was going to make a great manager.

"I thought you'd like to know," Cindy went on. "Mandy's doing great, and the doctors truly believe this operation will cure the problem until she's ready for a transplant. Tell Effie she's a saint."

Parker looked Effie's way. "Cindy says you're a saint."

Effie grinned and walked toward him. "She's wrong. I'm a clown."

She touched him between the legs as he sucked in a breath. "Anything wrong?" Cindy asked.

Effie kissed him, and Parker closed his eyes. "No. Everything's fine. Absolutely perfect."

THE EDITORS' CORNER

What do a cowboy, a straitlaced professor, a federal agent, and a wildlife photographer have in common? They're the sizzling men you'll meet in next month's LOVESWEPT lineup, and they're uniting with wonderful heroines for irresistible tales of passion and romance. Packed with emotion, these terrific stories are guaranteed to keep you enthralled. Enjoy!

Longtime romance favorite Karen Leabo begins the glorious BRIDES OF DESTINY series with **CALLIE'S COWBOY**, LOVESWEPT #806, a story of poignant magic, tender promises, and revealing truths. Sam Sanger had always planned to share his ranch and his future with Callie Calloway, but even in high school he understood that loving this woman might mean letting her go! When a fortune-teller hinted that her fate lay with Sam, Callie ran—afraid a life with Sam would mean sacrificing her dreams. Now, ten years later, she stops running long enough to wonder if Sam is the destiny she most desires. Displaying the style that has made her a #1 bestselling author, Karen Leabo explores the deep longings that lead us to love.

Warming hearts and tickling funny bones from start to finish, award-winner Jennifer Crusie creates her own fairy tale of love in **THE CINDERELLA DEAL,** LOVESWEPT #807. Linc Blaise needs the perfect fiancée to win his dream job, but finding a woman who'll be convincing in the charade seems impossible—until he hears Daisy Flattery charm her way out of a sticky situation! The bedazzling storyteller knows it'll be a snap playing a prim and proper lady to Linc's serious professor, but the pretense turns into a risky temptation when she discovers the vulnerable side Linc tries so hard to hide. Jennifer Crusie debuts in LOVESWEPT with an utterly charming story of opposites attracting.

Acclaimed author Laura Taylor provides a **SLIGHTLY SCANDALOUS** scenario for her memorable hero and heroine in her newest LOVESWEPT, #808. Trapped with a rugged stranger when a sudden storm stops an elevator between floors, Claire Duncan is shocked to feel the undeniable heat of attraction! In Tate Richmond she senses strength shadowed by a loneliness that echoes her own unspoken need. Vowing to explore the hunger that sparks between them, forced by unusual circumstances to resort to clandestine meetings, Tate draws her to him with tender ferocity. He has always placed honor above desire, kept himself safe in a world of constant peril, but once he's trusted his destiny to a woman of mystery, he can't live without her touch.

Laura Taylor packs quite a punch with this exquisite romance!

RaeAnne Thayne sets the mood with reckless passion and fierce destiny in **WILD STREAK,** LOVE-SWEPT #809. Keen Malone can't believe his ears when Meg O'Neill turns him down for a loan! Determined to make the cool beauty understand that his wildlife center is the mountain's only hope, he persuades her to tour the site. Meg can't deny the lush beauty of the land he loves, but how long can she fight the wild longing to run into his arms? RaeAnne Thayne creates a swirl of undeniable attraction in this classic romance of two strangers who discover they share the same fierce desire.

Happy reading!

With warmest wishes,

Beth de Guzman

Shauna Summers

Beth de Guzman   Shauna Summers

Senior Editor   Editor

P.S. Watch for these Bantam women's fiction titles coming in October. Praised by Amanda Quick as "an exciting find for romance readers everywhere," Elizabeth Elliott dazzles with **BETROTHED,** the much anticipated sequel to her debut novel, THE WAR-LORD. When Guy of Montague finds himself trapped in an engagement to Claudia, Baron Lonsdale's beautiful niece, his only thought is escape. But when she comes to his rescue, with the condition that he take her with him, he finds himself under her spell, willing to risk everything—even his life—to capture her heart. And don't miss **TAME THE WILD WIND** by Rosanne Bittner, the mistress of romantic frontier fiction. Half-breed Gabe Beaumont rides with a renegade Sioux band until a raid on a Wyoming stage post unites him with Faith Kelley. Together they will face their destinies and fight for their love against the shadows of their own wild hearts.

Be sure to see next month's LOVESWEPTs for a preview of these exceptional novels. And immediately following this page, preview the Bantam women's fiction titles on sale *now*!

Don't miss these extraordinary books
by your favorite Bantam authors

On sale in August:

AMANDA
by Kay Hooper

THE MARSHAL AND THE HEIRESS
by Patricia Potter

TEXAS LOVER
by Adrienne deWolfe

"Amanda seethes and sizzles. A fast-paced atmospheric tale that vibrates with tension, passion, and mystery."—Catherine Coulter

AMANDA

from bestselling author
Kay Hooper
now available in paperback

When a missing heiress to a vast fortune suddenly reappears, there's good reason for suspicion. After all, others before her had claimed to be Amanda Daulton; is this poised woman the genuine article or another impostor hoping to cash in? Unlike the family patriarch, others at the Southern mansion called Glory are not so easily swayed by Amanda's claim. They have too much at stake—enough, perhaps, to commit murder. . . .

July, 1975

Thunder rolled and boomed, echoing the way it did when a storm came over the mountains on a hot night, and the wind-driven rain lashed the trees and furiously pelted the windowpanes of the big house. The nine-year-old girl shivered, her cotton nightgown soaked and clinging to her, and her slight body was stiff as she stood in the center of the dark bedroom.

"Mama—"

"Shhhh! Don't, baby, don't make any noise. Just stand there, very still, and wait for me."

They called her baby often, her mother, her father, because she'd been so difficult to conceive and was so cherished once they had her. So beloved. That was why they had named her Amanda, her father had explained, lifting her up to ride upon his broad shoulders, because she was so perfect and so worthy of their love.

She didn't feel perfect now. She felt cold and emptied out and dreadfully afraid. And the sound of her mother's voice, so thin and desperate, frightened Amanda even more. The bottom had fallen out of her world so suddenly that she was still numbly bewildered and broken, and her big gray eyes followed her mother with the piteous dread of one who had lost everything except a last fragile, unspeakably precious tie to what had been.

Whispering between rumbles of thunder, she asked, "Mama, where will we go?"

"Away, far away, baby." The only illumination in the bedroom was provided by angry nature as lightning split the stormy sky outside, and Christine Daulton used the flashes to guide her in stuffing clothes into an old canvas duffel bag. She dared not turn on any lights, and the need to hurry was so fierce it nearly strangled her.

She hadn't room for them, but she pushed her journals into the bag as well because she had to have *something* of this place to take with her, and something of her life with Brian. *Oh, dear God, Brian* . . . She raked a handful of jewelry from the box on the dresser, tasting blood because she was biting her bottom lip to keep herself from screaming. There was no time, no time, she had to get Amanda away from here.

"Wait here," she told her daughter.

"No! Mama, please—"

"Shhhh! All right, Amanda, come with me—but you have to be quiet." Moments later, down the hall in her daughter's room, Christine fumbled for more clothing and thrust it into the bulging bag. She helped the silent, trembling girl into dry clothing, faded jeans and a tee shirt. "Shoes?"

Amanda found a pair of dirty sneakers and shoved her feet into them. Her mother grasped her hand and led her from the room, both of them consciously tiptoeing. Then, at the head of the stairs, Amanda suddenly let out a moan of anguish and tried to pull her hand free. "Oh, I *can't*—"

"Shhhh," Christine warned urgently. "Amanda—"

Even whispering, Amanda's voice held a desperate intensity. "Mama, please, Mama, I have to get something—I can't leave it here, please, Mama—it'll only take a second—"

She had no idea what could be so precious to her daughter, but Christine wasn't about to drag her down the stairs in this state of wild agitation. The child was already in shock, a breath away from absolute hysteria. "All right, but hurry. And *be quiet*."

As swift and silent as a shadow, Amanda darted back down the hallway and vanished into her bedroom. She reappeared less than a minute later, shoving something into the front pocket of her jeans. Christine didn't pause to find out what was so important that Amanda couldn't bear to leave it behind; she simply grabbed her daughter's free hand and continued down the stairs.

The grandfather clock on the landing whirred and bonged a moment before they reached it, announcing in sonorous tones that it was two A.M. The sound was too familiar to startle either of them, and they hurried on without pause. The front door was still open, as they'd left it, and Christine didn't bother to pull it shut behind them as they went through to the wide porch.

The wind had blown rain halfway over the porch to the door, and Amanda dimly heard her shoes squeak on the wet stone. Then she ducked her head against the rain and stuck close to her mother as they raced for the car parked several yards away. By the time she was sitting in the front seat watching her mother fumble with the keys, Amanda was soaked again and shivering, despite a temperature in the seventies.

The car's engine coughed to life, and its headlights stabbed through the darkness and sheeting rain to illuminate the graveled driveway. Amanda turned her head to the side as the car jolted toward the paved road, and she caught her breath when she saw a light bobbing far away between the house and the stables, as if someone was running with a flashlight. Running toward the car that, even then, turned onto the paved road and picked up speed as it left the house behind.

Quickly, Amanda turned her gaze forward again, rubbing her cold hands together, swallowing hard as sickness rose in her aching throat. "Mama? We can't come back, can we? We can't ever come back?"

The tears running down her ashen cheeks almost but not quite blinding her, Christine Daulton replied, "No, Amanda. We can't ever come back."

"One of the romance genre's finest talents."
—Romantic Times

From
Patricia Potter
bestselling author of *DIABLO*
comes

THE MARSHAL AND THE HEIRESS

When U.S. Marshal Ben Masters became Sarah Ann's guardian, he didn't know she was the lost heir to a Scottish estate—or that her life would soon be in danger. Now, instead of hunting down a gun-toting outlaw, he faces an aristocratic household bitterly divided by ambition. And not even falling in love with Sarah Ann's beautiful young aunt could keep her from being a suspect in Ben's eyes.

How do you tell a four-year-old girl that her mother is dead?

U.S. Marshal Ben Masters worried over the question as he stood on the porch of Mrs. Henrietta Culworthy's small house. Then, squaring his shoulders, he knocked. He wished he really believed he was doing the right thing. What in God's name did a man like him, a man who'd lived with guns and violence for the past eight years, have to offer an orphaned child?

Mary May believed in you. The thought raked through his heart. He felt partially responsible for her death. He had stirred a pot without considering the consequences. In bringing an end to an infamous outlaw hideout, he had been oblivious to those caught in the cross fire. The fact that Mary May had been involved with the outlaws didn't assuage his conscience.

Sarah. Promise you'll take care of Sarah. He would never forget Mary May's last faltering words.

Ben rapped again on the door of the house. Mrs. Culworthy should be expecting him. She had been looking after Sarah Ann for the past three years, but now she had to return east to care for a brother. She had already postponed her trip once, agreeing to wait until Ben had wiped out the last remnants of an outlaw band and fulfilled a promise to the former renegade named Diablo.

The door opened. Mrs. Culworthy's wrinkled face appeared, sagging slightly with relief. Had she worried that he would not return? He sure as hell had thought about it. He'd thought about a lot of things, like where he might find another suitable home for Sarah Ann. But then he would never be sure she was being raised properly. By God, he owed Mary May.

"Sarah Ann?" he asked Mrs. Culworthy.

"In her room." The woman eyed him hopefully. "You *are* going to take her."

He nodded.

"What about your job?"

"I'm resigning. I used to be a lawyer. Thought I would hang up my shingle in Denver."

A smile spread across Mrs. Culworthy's face. "Thank heaven for you. I love that little girl. I would take her if I could, but—"

"I know you would," he said gently. "But she'll be safe with me." He hoped that was true. He hesitated. "She doesn't know yet, does she? About her mother?"

Mrs. Culworthy shook her head.

Just then, a small head adorned with reddish curls

and green eyes peered around the door. Excitement lit the gamin face. "Mama's here!"

Pain thrust through Ben. Of course, Sarah Ann would think her mother had arrived. Mary May had been here with him just a few weeks ago.

"Uncle Ben," the child said, "where's Mama?"

He wished Mrs. Culworthy had already told her. He was sick of being the bearer of bad news, and never more so than now.

He dropped to one knee and held out a hand to the little girl. "She's gone to heaven," Ben said.

She approached slowly, her face wrinkling in puzzlement; then she looked questioningly at Mrs. Culworthy. The woman dissolved into tears. Ben didn't know whether Sarah Ann understood what was being said, but she obviously sensed that something was very wrong. The smile disappeared and her underlip started to quiver.

Ben's heart quaked. He had guarded that battered part of him these past years, but there were no defenses high enough, or thick enough, to withstand a child's tears.

He held out his arms, not sure Sarah Ann knew him well enough to accept his comfort. But she walked into his embrace, and he hugged her, stiffly at first. Unsure. But then her need overtook his uncertainty, and his grip tightened.

"You asked me once if I were your papa," he said. "Would you like me to be?"

Sarah Ann looked up at him. "Isn't Mama coming back?"

He shook his head. "She can't, but she loved you so much she asked me to take care of you. If that's all right with you?"

Sarah Ann turned to Mrs. Culworthy. "I want to stay with you, Cully."

"You can't, Pumpkin," Mrs. Culworthy said tenderly. "I have to go east, but Mr. Masters will take good care of you. Your mother thought so, too."

"Where is heaven? Can't I go, too?"

"Someday," Ben said slowly. "And she'll be waiting for you, but right now I need you. I need someone to take care of me, too, and your mama thought we could take care of each other."

It was true, he suddenly realized. He did need someone to love. His life had been empty for so long.

Sarah Ann probably had much to offer him.

But what did he have to offer her?

Sarah Ann put her hand to his cheek. The tiny fingers were incredibly soft—softer than anything he'd ever felt—and gentle. She had lost everything, yet she was comforting him.

He hugged her close for a moment, and then he stood. Sarah Ann's hand crept into his. Trustingly. And Ben knew he would die before ever letting anything bad happen to her again.

TEXAS LOVER

by

Adrienne deWolfe

author of *TEXAS OUTLAW*

To Texas Ranger Wes Rawlins, settling a property dispute should be no trickier than peeling potatoes—even if it does involve a sheriff's cousin and a headstrong schoolmarm on opposite camps. But Wes quickly learns there's more to the matter than meets the eye. The only way to get at the truth is from the inside. So posing as a carpenter, the lawman uncovers more than he bargains for in a feisty beauty and her house full of orphans.

"Sons of thunder."

Rorie rarely resorted to such unladylike outbursts, but the strain of her predicament was wearing on her. She had privately conceded she could not face Hannibal Dukker with the same laughable lack of shooting skill she had displayed for Wes Rawlins. So, swallowing her great distaste for guns—and the people who solved their problems with them—she had forced herself to ride out to the woods early, before the children arrived for their lessons, to practice her marksmanship.

It was a good thing she had done so.

She had just fired her sixth round, her *sixth round*, for heaven's sake, and that abominable whiskey bottle still sat untouched on the top of her barrel. If she had been a fanciful woman—which she most assuredly was not—she might have imagined that impudent vessel was trying to provoke her. Why, it hadn't rattled once when her bullets whizzed by. And the long rays of morning sun had fired it a bright and frolicsome green. If there was one thing she couldn't abide, it was a frolicsome whiskey bottle.

Her mouth set in a grim line, she fished in the pocket of her pinafore for more bullets.

Thus occupied, Rorie didn't immediately notice the tremor of the earth beneath her boots. She didn't ascribe anything unusual to her nag's snorting or the way Daisy stomped her hoof and tossed her head. The beast was chronically fractious.

Soon, though, Rorie detected the sound of thrashing, as if a powerful animal were breaking through the brush around the clearing. Her heart quickened, but she tried to remain calm. After all, bears were hardly as brutish as their hunters liked to tell. And any other wild animal with sense would turn tail and run once it got wind of her human scent—not to mention a whiff of her gunpowder.

Still, it might be wise to start reloading. . . .

A bloodcurdling whoop shook her hands. She couldn't line up a single bullet with its chamber. She thought to run, but there was nowhere to hide, and Daisy was snapping too viciously to mount.

Suddenly the sun winked out of sight. A horse, a *mammoth* horse with fiery eyes and steaming nostrils, sailed toward her over the barrel. She tried to scream, but it lodged in her throat as an "eek." All she could do was stand there, jaw hanging, knees knocking, and remember the unfortunate schoolmaster, Ichabod Crane.

Only her horseman had a head.

A red head, to be exact. And he carried it above his shoulders, rather than tucked under his arm.

"God a'mighty! Miss Aurora!"

The rider reined in so hard that his gelding reared, shrilling in indignation. Her revolver slid from her fingers. She saw a peacemaker in the rider's fist, and she thought again about running.

"It's me, ma'am. Wes Rawlins," he called, then cursed as his horse wheeled and pawed.

She blinked uncertainly, still poised to flee. He didn't look like the dusty longrider who'd drunk from her well the previous afternoon. His hair was sleek and short, and his cleft chin was bare of all but morning stubble. Although he did still wear the mustache, it was the gunbelt that gave him away. She recognized the double holsters before she recognized his strong, sculpted features.

He managed to subdue his horse before it could bolt back through the trees. "Are you all right, ma'am?" He hastily dismounted, releasing his reins to ground-hitch the gelding. "Uh-oh." He peered into her face. "You aren't gonna faint or anything, are you?"

She snapped erect, mortified by the very suggestion. "Certainly not. I've never been sick a day in my life. And swooning is for invalids."

"Sissies, too," he agreed solemnly.

He ran an appreciative gaze over her hastily piled hair and down her crisply pressed pinafore to her mud-spattered boots. She felt the blood surge to her cheeks. Masking her discomfort, she planted both fists on her hips.

"*Mister* Rawlins. What on earth is the matter with you, tearing around the countryside like that? You frightened the devil out of my horse!"

"I'm real sorry, ma'am. I never meant to give

your, er, *horse* such a fright. But you see, I heard gun-shots. And since there's nothing out this way except the Boudreau homestead, I thought you might be having trouble."

"Trouble?" She felt her heart flutter. Had he heard something of Dukker's intentions?

"Well, sure. Yesterday, the way you had those children running for cover, I thought you might be expecting some." He folded his arms across his chest. "Are you?"

The directness of his question—and his gaze—was unsettling. He no longer reminded her of a lion. Today he was a fox, slick and clever, with a dash of sly charm thrown in to confuse her. She hastily bolstered her defenses.

"Did it ever occur to you, Mr. Rawlins, that Shae might be out here shooting rabbits?"

"Nope. Never thought I'd find you here, either. Not that I mind, ma'am. Not one bit. You see, I'm the type who likes surprises. Especially pleasant ones."

She felt her face grow warmer. She wasn't used to flattery. Her husband had been too preoccupied with self-pity to spare many kind words for her in the last two years of their marriage.

"Well," she said, "I never expected to see you out here either, Mr. Rawlins."

"Call me Wes."

She forced herself to ignore his winsome smile. "In truth, sir, I never thought to see you again."

"Why's that?"

"Let's be honest, Mr. Rawlins. You are no carpen-ter."

He chuckled. She found herself wondering which had amused him more: her accusation or her refusal to use his Christian name.

"You have to give a feller a chance, Miss Aurora. You haven't even seen my handiwork yet."

"I take it you've worked on barns before?"

"Sure. Fences too. My older brothers have a ranch up near Bandera Pass. Zack raises cattle. Cord raises kids. I try to raise a little thunder now and then, but they won't let me." He winked. "That's why I had to ride south."

She felt a smile tug at her lips. She was inclined to believe a part of his story, the part about him rebelling against authority.

"You aren't gonna make me bed down again in these woods, are you, ma'am? 'Cause Two-Step is awful fond of hay."

He managed to look woeful, in spite of the impish humor lighting his eyes. She realized then just how practiced his roguery was. Wary again, she searched his gaze, trying to find some hint of the truth. Why hadn't he stayed at the hotel in town? Or worse, at the dance hall? She felt better knowing he hadn't spent his free time exploiting an unfortunate young whore, but she still worried that his reasons for sleeping alone had more to do with empty pockets than any nobility of character. What would Rawlins do if Dukker offered to hire his guns?

Maybe feeding and housing Rawlins was more prudent than driving him off. Boarding him could steer him away from Dukker's dangerous influence, and Shae could genuinely use the help on the barn.

"Very well, Mr. Rawlins. I shall withhold judgment on your carpentry skills until you've had a chance to prove yourself."

"Why, that's right kind of you, ma'am."

She felt her cheeks grow warm again. His lilting drawl had the all-too-disturbing tendency to make her feel uncertain and eighteen again.

"I suppose you'll want to ride on to the house now," she said. "It's a half-mile farther west. Shae is undoubtedly awake and can show you what to do." She inclined her head. "Good morning."

Except for a cannily raised eyebrow, he didn't budge.

Rorie fidgeted. She was unused to her dismissals going unheeded. She was especially unused to a young man regarding her as if she had just made the most delightful quip of the season.

Hoping he would go away if she ignored him, she stooped to retrieve her gun. He reached quickly to help. She was so stunned when he crouched before her, his corded thighs straining beneath the fabric of his blue jeans, that she leaped up, nearly butting her head against his. He chuckled.

"Do I make you nervous, ma'am?"

"Certainly not." Her ears burned at the lie. "Whatever makes you think that?"

"Well . . ." Still squatting, he scooped bullets out of the bluebonnets that rose like sapphire spears around her hem. "I was worried you might be trying to get rid of me again."

"I—I only thought that Shae was expecting you," she stammered, hastily backing away. There was something disconcerting—not to mention titillating—about a man's bronzed fingers snaking through the grass and darting so near to the unmentionables one wore beneath one's skirt.

"Shae's not expecting me yet, ma'am. The sun's too low in the sky." Rawlins straightened leisurely. "I figure I've got a half hour, maybe more, before I report to the barn. Just think, Miss Aurora, that gives us plenty of time to get acquainted."

On sale in September:

TAME THE WILD HEART

by Rosanne Bittner

BETROTHED

by Elizabeth Elliott